FIC   Vac    D0569759

          The axe.

$12.95

DATE			

The A...

》》》》》》》》》》 《《《《《《《《《《

Ludvík Vaculík

The AXE

TRANSLATED FROM THE CZECH BY

MARIAN SLING

NORTHWESTERN UNIVERSITY PRESS

EVANSTON, ILLINOIS

》》》》》》》》》》》 《《《《《《《《《《《

Northwestern University Press

Evanston, Illinois 60208-4210

Originally published in Czechoslovakia under the title *Das Beil*. Copyright ©
1966 by Ludvík Vaculík. English translation copyright © 1973 by André
Deutsch Limited. First published in the U.S. by Harper & Row, Publishers.
Northwestern University Press edition published 1994 by arrangement with
Ludvík Vaculík. All rights reserved.

Printed in the United States of America

ISBN 0-8101-1018-0

Library of Congress Cataloging-in-Publication Data

Vaculík, Ludvík.

    [Sekyra. English]

    The axe / Ludvík Vaculík ; translated from the Czech by Marian
Sling.

        p. cm. — (European classics)

    ISBN 0-8101-1018-0 (pbk: alk. paper)

    I. Sling, Marian. II. Title. III. Series: European classics
(Evanston, Ill.)

PG5039.32.A2S413 1994

891.8'635—dc20   94-10931

                                        CIP

The following names have been given
phonetic spellings in the text in order to
facilitate their pronunciation:

Pukys	Pukysh
Mrs Pukysova	Pukyshova
Trencin	Trenchin
Kanur	Kanyur
Eliska	Elishka
Senkerick	Shenkerik
Decin	Dechin
Drahuse	Drahushe
Zbyszek	Zbyshek
Vrsatec	Vrshatets

I

This was to be my first visit to my brother the bus driver – but, of course, nobody really knows about that brother of mine. Well, I was ten when suddenly I found myself saddled with the boring job of having to rock his cradle now and then. I even remember driving our goats to the stream the morning he was born; Tonda had arrived there before me, and I said to him: "Guess what's happened!" – and he said: "It's a brother, isn't it?" I was really taken aback at Tonda saying that. By the time this brother of mine had reached the age of five, I had gone out into the world, by the time he had reached my ten years, I was twenty, and could a brother like that interest me? I was more inclined to count him among the minor household accessories. When I went back for holiday weekends I learnt no more than some general comments from our parents about the rotten marks he got at school and that he was bad at minding the goats. So, while in a rational way I was aware that, among other things, I had this brother, the experience went no deeper. And it is my considered opinion that only brothers who are close in age are really born as brothers; when the age gap is bigger, they can only become brothers in later life.

For the first time, then, I was about to visit my driver brother – but, come to think of it, you may wonder how he came to be a driver. Well, even I don't know that. When he rang my doorbell in Prague one day and I saw him standing there all trussed up in the Road Transport uniform, I thought he was trying to have me on in a big way. Nobody had bothered to tell me that this brother of mine was to work in road transport. Only when, round the corner from the block where I live, I saw the monstrous removal van, that yellow peril of our winding motorways, did I really accept the fact that the brat who used to wet his pants was now a van driver. He was still in his cradle that time I dropped a loaf of bread on his face because it slipped out of my hands as I was trying to cut it. "Hullo there," said my brother twenty-five years later, "can you put us up for the night?" And he brought a gang of removal men into the kitchen – so much for how he became a driver.

So I was going to visit this brother for the first time – but you may ask why I attribute such importance to the visit. I don't really. I just keep hitting on something that needs explaining. In fact, my brother had invited me at least twenty times, until it became almost impossible to go there without making an occasion of it. For some years he had not been to see me either. Having managed to get transferred from freight to passenger transport, his trips to Prague had stopped. So now we only see each other about once a year, when visiting our sister who occupies the family cottage. I go there for my holidays, and he simply turns up now and then. Sometimes our visits happen to coincide and then, for an evening, the three of us are together. Out in the garden the summer apples drop from the trees and our sister says: "Well, boys, let's have some news, now there are two of you here!" She gets on with a pile of washing-up that has accumulated over the days when she came home late from work. Her husband makes a silent fourth, sitting sideways at the table under the window to consume a biggish joint from a smallish rabbit because he has just come off the shift. Three yards from our window the bus rattles past, packed with villagers coming home from the factory for a few hours' sleep in their cottages. My brother and I have no news, or more accurately, whatever the news may be, it is the same in any part of our country, so that every sister knows it.

Nevertheless, my brother says with a smile: "Have you heard the news? They've plucked a bald goose!" He can laugh now, he feels fine now, but it was no laughing matter twenty-five years ago when I scalded his hand with rabbit soup. How did it happen, you ask? Mother took the pot off the stove, she told us to put out the plates, we put them out, then my sister said she wanted the head, our youngest brother cried and the older one laughed at him, I wanted the head for myself, I ran off with it into the yard and locked myself in the lavatory, where it was more peaceful. Just then Mother poured out the soup and our youngest brother plonked his hand right into it. So that's how I scalded his hand. It was a Sunday. Dad was in Persia.

Shakhabdullazim 19/VII 1936

My dear son,

Here around the cement works, where the surroundings are rocky, there were many vultures two months ago. Now they have flown off somewhere and there are falcons and eagles. There is vermin of all kinds. If you sit by the stream for five minutes – to relieve yourself perhaps – you can see in the water, if you keep quiet, rats that are smaller than ours, but the same colour, and also long black creatures bigger than rats, but I don't know what they are. Also you can observe numbers of snakes going upstream and down. Out in the desert there are porcupines, tortoises beside the watercourses, and altogether there is much vermin in this Persian land. Poor people – lice, the shits, malaria, dysentery, capitalists and death. Two days ago two Czechoslovaks met their death, we didn't even know, for the bosses said nothing, and three weeks ago one engineer. Our luck is running out it seems. I shall look forward to my home, to my family and to our hills which do not kill; the forests welcome a man, the trees nod their heads and sigh. One is safe, even at night, in our woods. Otherwise I am well. Tomorrow the emperor of this land (Mr Shah) is to visit us on the building site. Mother has not even written to say how she gets the money, whether in time or late, but I suppose it is always late if she still has none. St Anne's brings chill mornings, and before this letter reaches you the wind will be blowing across the stubble and I can't think who will pick the apples and damsons for you.

"Don't go!" Mother pleaded a quarter of a century ago. But we, unflinching, shouldered our rucksacks. It was high time. Any minute the moon would be rising over the hill; a quarter of a century ago all the sky on that side was tautly yellow.

"Leave the boy at home, at least!" But I knew he wouldn't leave me when I wanted to go with him. Dad and I were team mates; we crushed her pitiful moaning beneath our stony resolve to go our own way. She would shiver for two hours there at home, and for no reason, because nothing ever happened to us.

Cautiously, we stole up above the barns. As we crossed the railway line, the gravel crunched rather noisily under my feet and Dad looked back with a "Chr-i-st" – I thought we would climb to the path along the ridge, but we kept on up the side of the hill, hard going with no path; some dogs started barking down by the brook and I was afraid people would guess it was us. I knew now why we were not taking the field path: we would have stood out against the skyline as clearly as in daylight. Dad was a good leader! The moon had risen.

It was a long way from the village to where we joined the path a quarter of a century ago. It is really a tangle of paths, furrowed by the torrents of spring and then smoothed over by the iron-shod wheels of waggons braking down the hill. There is a classical beauty in these wheels and the clay in their tracks glistens like iron. The dusty white path drove hard towards the great hill over which tomorrow's sun would greet us. Every detail is familiar here. Even in the dark we know the owner of this field, of that meadow, and we can always say that none belong to us. For we have nothing but our cottage, newly built, its walls still unplastered. The three apple trees in our garden will start bearing fruit in many years' time, in times as yet beyond our ken.

Out in the garden, apples are falling in the darkness, our sister is washing the pans, her husband eating his supper. Sitting on the old ottoman, elbows propped on his knees, my brother wrinkles his shiny, swarthy brow, smiling softly in contentment. He has no idea how disappointed Dad was that his eyes were brown, because Mother had written that they were blue, but by the time Dad got home from Persia those eyes had turned brown.

We had reached the meeting of the waters and that is a lovely place. Two streams flow down from the rolling meadows to murmur unseen beneath the bushes screening the deep gulley, down and away, their glory known to none. With sure step we trod through grass moist with the light fall of early dew, until we came to a corner where fear overtook me. It was a hummocky paddock – a place I knew perfectly well by daylight. The thickets hemming it in on all sides are known in these parts as holts. Lime, oak, hazel, dogwood. I do not want to mention the name of the man who owned that paddock. Its trees were ancient and twisted. Only its molehills were ever new. It had sunk so deep, so long ago, into the ancient glen, that a maiden might herd a cow there for thirty years, yet time would never track them down, either of them. But for all that, the moon was shining, the stream purled smoothly in its deep channel, and the immeasurable hush of the night sighed faintly over the land as I whispered:

"Dad, what am I to do?"

He looked round, put down his rucksack, bent towards me, breathing in a smoky croak:

"Keep a good look-out!"

I shivered. Dad shinned up a tree. I had the feeling that while my eyes were glued on the path, somebody was waiting to pounce upon us from the stream. On turning sharply towards the stream, I imagined the unknown coming at us from the path. It took me a quarter of an hour to collect my wits sufficiently to realize that nobody could get at us from the stream because he would be sure to come a cropper in the narrow gorge, with a resounding crash at that; while the chances of anyone coming along the path were a thousand times less than in the daytime and, in any case, the man never passed this way for weeks on end because he had plenty of better fields. The bark of the tree crunched under Dad's boot. Every time he pulled an apple it sounded like a shot. Gradually, however, I grew bolder; reaching for the lower branches where I was hiding, I started carefully picking apples and stowing them in my knapsack. And now open your mouth quietly in a wide ah. Then breathe out, a long, supple, tender breath. Mindful that this breath is yours, confess to yourself that your breath is dear to you. Well, that is approximately the sound of a windless night, a sound compounded of the silent wafting in a million trees on the hills and in the gardens, and of the imperceptible motion of the stars across the heavens.

Sliding from the tree, the intrepid leader bent over me; he laughed at the twelve apples in my knapsack, and with a few swift plucks he filled it for me. His touch was unerring because he could identify the fruit at a glance in the intricate silhouette of dark leaves against a lighter sky.

We made sure we had not left anything; I patted the grass where I had been squatting and counting everything in my pockets. That I had already learnt to do. Dad gathered a few fallen twigs and threw them into the holt.

Again he led the way. I thought about Mother. So now we had another sin to our names! Dad glanced back now and again, pausing for me to catch up. I had still not mastered the art of walking as he did, without the metal studs on my boots striking sparks from the stones, and without squelching whenever we happened on a muddy patch. Actually, I have not learnt it yet, time flies, and the worst of it is that now I shall never learn.

"Dad, suppose there'd been a thief there and he'd recognized us?"

Without giving much thought to the matter, he said:

"It's Kismet."

We arrived home, the dogs were still barking at the moon. I could see Dad was pleased that Mother had waited up for us. Only she hadn't waited for us, she was simply doing the mending.

"Heavens above, as fast as I sew it it's all in holes again!"

But Dad needed to show off. He made out that the apples must be put immediately into boxes in the attic and that Mother must help him. But she took one look at our green, unappetizing fruit and exclaimed:

"Oh my! What little wretches!"

All of which happened one moonlit night in September.

One black winter night, again, it happened that someone cried out for help. In those days our cottage stood alone at the end of the village. The road running past the door was lined by an avenue of giant linden trees, the darkness beneath them was solid black. On both sides of this road, under the trees, stretched an unbroken line of barns. Barn upon barn, never since have I seen such a singular street. To walk there was to be seized with fear and terror, for which reason I never walked there but always bolted past, reaching the doorstep a second ahead of the pursuing fiend. And suddenly, out of that blackness came the cry: "He-e-elp!"

It came from the field where the water frothed on the

mill-wheel, from the heart and womb of darkness itself, from the clumps of fearful pitch where, if a light ever shone, it shone from a tiny window in the mill.

"He-e-elp!" came the piteous cry, and help there was none. A long wait ensued before a few lanterns started winking in the distance. And next morning we heard about the accident. A drunkard walking beside the mill-stream had fallen in such a manner that his legs stayed on one bank, his head on the other. Consequently, his arse sagged deep in the icy water. Awakening to his helpless plight, he was seized with terror.

One Saturday morning someone hammered on our window.

"Uncle, let us in!"

We woke up.

"Aunt, for God's sake, open the door!"

Into the hall tumbled two of my cousins from Tarandova, and they were bleeding. Tarandova is the village next to ours and it is the cradle of Dad's clan. The clan had long been at war with another Tarandova clan, and that night the two sides had come to blows at a dance in our village. The battle had spilled over from the dance hall into the adjacent farmyards, even into the byres. One of my cousins had pulled a heavy iron rib from a cow-yoke and with this weapon had warded off the onslaught so fiercely that he had taken a terrible thrashing before escaping by the skin of his teeth from the enraged band of foes. The first thing the Tarandova cousins did when they had burst into our cottage was to blow out the lamp; hubbub and curses thudded past the windows. When that was over, the light went up again and the cruel wounds were bathed in a basin.

And one night, a lonely barn near us went up in flames. Our cottage was soaked, thanks to the preventive diligence of the firemen. The apples, baked in the straw of the gutted barn to an alluring colour, stank horribly of burnt shingles.

One night a mighty gust stripped the roofs off the barns, but our roof came to no harm. What better augury could one desire?

Our goats, too, insisted on having their kids at night.

Therefore, taking it all in all, it is my desire that night should be a time of perfect darkness and no illuminated signs should shine. There are professionals who deem it necessary to edify the nation even at night, a task the enormity of which is simply ludicrous. A true Titan would be the man who could arrange for us all to sleep at night. But, nowadays, a proper night is probably as rare as a nation that dares to live without neon lights, or simply to go its own way. Night, night should be the raindrops in the leaves, or the scrabbling of branches on the roof-tops. At night let thieves break in and steal, let the lads brawl outside the taverns, but let nothing else shove its nose in, or else we'll take a running jump at it, which is what it will come to one day, in any case!

And so it was nearly midnight when our sister suggested that we have some tea. We drank it, all four of us, sister, brother-in-law, the driver brother and I. Our middle brother didn't drink tea with us, of course, because he is in Slovakia. We had bread and redcurrant jam with it, only our sister ate a dry roll. Meantime, a lorry made approximately its fifth run past our window with coal from the station to the factory; they never rest even at night.

"And what about fuel, have you got enough?" my driver brother enquired.

Our sister laughed, while her husband said:

"Well ... yes. They didn't deliver the coal we'd ordered, you know, because they hadn't any. Then, when they did have some, you know, our order had lapsed. But wood," he added, with an impassive shrug, "there's plenty of that."

"Really? You've got enough wood?" I asked.

"Oh yes," with an impassive shrug, "I took part of my holiday in the winter to do a bit of lumbering."

"Well, having the wood in is the main thing," said the driver brother.

"But just you tell them," my sister urged her husband, "tell them how much we had to pay the carter, let alone anything else. Five hundred crowns the carter cost us, and we had to plead with him to do it at that." She brandished her roll as she spoke.

But my brother-in-law merely muttered something and then proceeded to drink up his tea.

Before we all turned in, my brother and I stood up against the fence behind the cottage for a necessary moment. Apples were dropping from the full-grown trees, that's true. But what's the use when, in place of a babbling brook alive with fish, there's a babbling sewer, and where the mill window should, by rights, be shining into the darkness you now see block upon block of tenement windows. All these new houses belong to the factory; my father got that factory built so he wouldn't have to go to Persia. Before them, even the avenue of mighty lindens crashed to the ground. And one night, well one night the barns, too, went up in flames. I have my own theory about these manifestations, and I feel the need to talk about it now. But my driver brother's primary need is a place to live in. Anyhow, he's too young for theories like that. I, however, am no longer too young. I am old enough to discuss them even with Dad. Unfortunately, Dad is not alive enough any more.

2

I let up the blind in the kitchen. My brother the driver sat up with a jerk on the ottoman.

"I haven't missed the train, have I?"

"Look, there's no train. Stay here!"

The cat, which had come in with me, jumped on his bare knee. He stroked her and called her a rascal.

I pulled the electric ring out of the washstand cupboard, put it on a stool and plugged it in. My brother corrected me; he lifted the ring to slip an old blackened board underneath.

The minute Dad noticed the hole that had been burnt in the stool, he grabbed the ring, he grabbed the stool, flung open the door and threw the whole lot over the fence into a snowdrift. My two brothers stood open-mouthed, not lifting a finger, until the little one started laughing. Mother's warning cry was no more than a belated bleat, because in a trice the boy was in the snow-drift, too. The other brother, the one who is now in Slovakia, but at that time was sitting on the wood-box, followed these events with an ominous cloud on his dark young brow; then he pattered barefoot to the door: "He shan't stay there!" he commanded. Whereupon he climbed over the fence to pick his little brother out of the snow. About this incident my memory is blank. In fact, I have a suspicion that for many long years my memory has been diligently censoring incidents of this nature on the mean and overworked pretext of deferring to higher interests.

We spread our bread with butter and redcurrant jam,

sitting one on each side of the table by the window, under which a lorry was engaged in depositing a load of iron pipes at the municipal workshop standing on the site of the barn whose doors I used to know by heart, while in the parlour my brother-in-law was still asleep because he was working the afternoon shift. Each of the clocks in the kitchen showed a different time.

After breakfast we stepped outside that cottage now doomed to extinction. Picking up some yellow apples, we wiped the mud from them in the damp grass. Over the fence we could see houses, between them stacks of wood, alternately – stacks of houses and stacks of wood.

"Plenty of wood!" my brother announced in the tone of a man wedded to the grassy lowlands.

"If you'd stay till after lunch, we could pop up the hill there," I suggested, suddenly realizing that in the sixty years of our combined lives we had never once done anything together.

"If I stayed till after lunch, mate, there'd be the devil to pay, because after lunch I have to start a turn of duty, see."

"Well, you wouldn't start," I ventured.

"If I didn't start, that would be worse still, because then I'd never get put on a regular route."

"I thought you'd got one."

"I've got sweet bugger all," he explained patiently, "I'm just a stop-gap when someone's sick or on holiday. There are three of us in that game and only one of us can get the route."

Returning to the house, he draped his jacket over his hefty shoulders, saying:

"Look here, you come along with me. What keeps you here? Chickenshit, I reckon."

"Just now it's no good, but I'll be coming soon!"

He stepped up to me.

"Know what you are, brother?"

"What, brother?"

"A swine, brother."

With that, we set off for the station, because we were not sure about the exact time of the train and all the clocks in the kitchen showed different times, according to when they had been bought. The station is built like a log cabin, its beams creak all the time. The greasy floor smells, the telegraph clicks outside the window, the sharp gravel on the platform crunches under the wheels of the handcart as they bring Dad's basket and suitcase. Mother stands gazing at the mouth of the tunnel, no, she is looking at the collar of Dad's new ulster, there's no sense in saying anything now, straighten his tie maybe, but he has reached across her hand to adjust the knot himself, and only today is it dawning on me that really she is young and I am actually a year older than him, how on earth will they live?

Shakhabdullazim 25/IV 1936

My dears!

That is my greeting to those for thought of whom I cannot sleep. The cottage has not fallen down and the gates still shut, nor is it probable that the devil has taken the creditors, and it is therefore necessary that I am here. But my life is plagued by the uncertainty about what is happening at home. I am still alive, and yet as if dead, since no one writes to me. I have not read anything since leaving the Republic, and I cannot read anything. Let it not be that I should accustom myself to separation, for here the consequences would be tragic. At least I have that basket of yours and in it still the rusks from grandma and bread not spoilt, so I have something from home. Who will help you, my dearest, when your hour comes? I often think of that. I wonder what the letter will bring? If I do not receive it, I shall know the worst. I am so very sorry for you all. When my spirit fails, I can only calm myself by saying: You dolt, what would you do at home, and if you do anything, what would you earn? And that is all for today, with kisses for all my dearest ones, I must go to bed. Dear wife, be mindful that my children do not forget me. May Providence have mercy upon us . . . And now may the gods cast their mantle around me in my joy, I have received the letter, today on Sunday evening at nine o'clock. I thank you, my dearest, that you have given me a son although I would have wished a daughter for you. Now that I know you are alive, I shall feel happier and I shall save, I was just about to spend that 100 Real. Why, I have debts with every second person in CSR, that is why I took to my heels. Let them go to Iran to earn money, those who want to, here the roads are covered in dust to make them soft for the asses and the camels. About the way they are pressing you, just say you have no money, and that's that. One has just turned one's back, and already they have started and I am still alive, what if I should be no more. It grieves me. And now, my dear one, I must go to sleep. I kiss my family and the new citizen of the world.

The diesel-car arrived, the new citizen of the world got into it, he gave me a last nod from the window and departed into the tunnel. And there, at the bend where it is darkest, my two younger brothers stationed themselves thirty paces apart and started the game they had been looking forward to: groping blindly for stones between the sleepers, they bombarded each other, and the black hole resounded with their rapturous roars.

"You never knew about that, did you, brother? And as for Dad, you could only let him know a quarter of what we were up to, because the way he was, he could have killed us."

"Tell me about the way he was," I spoke anxiously.

My brother went up to the wooden shed and ran his palm over the blackened side, feeling for something.

"Have you fed the rabbits?" Dad asked as he hammered the blade of the scythe.

"Yes," answered the brother in Slovakia.

"You shouldn't have!" cried our crafty Dad.

"But I didn't," shouted our brother.

And the deep dent marks the spot where the hammer struck. Our brother, who had actually fed the rabbits, succeeded in jumping aside, so that he is now in Slovakia. This dialogue had been Dad's favourite joke until our brother decided to play up to him that day.

The incidents they recall are often so different to mine that I sometimes wonder if they come from the same cottage. In the cottage I remember, the father used to lick his sons' wounds, for saliva is healing. Be mindful, my dear wife, that my children do not forget me.

Slowly I walked down the hill from the station. Lorries were still carting coal to the factory. An old body was gratefully gathering into her bag the larger of the pieces that had fallen by the wayside. She gave me a scared look. The road runs down, not steeply, so that in winter it could be used only by the slender shop-bought sleds, because the heavy kind made by the carpenter were not so good, and with advancing age I suppose I shall have to learn to tell people that they were no good at all. I am sorry about that.

My brother, who is now on the train and will not read even when he has left his native hills for the insipid plains, may really believe that I am occupying myself by and large with chickenshit, because he has no reason to know what a lot I have to do, things I don't know how to do and cannot do, including those that are forbidden. For many years I have been mustering the moral strength to do them; at one end I gather my resolve, and at the other it trickles away through the chinks in my character which, as I grow older, I see are becoming chronic. Yet a man should really do the best things in his life quickly, while he still has some good in him. The insoluble dilemma is, alas, that what is good should be wise, and wisdom arrives at a time when we have long since lost the necessary resolution and when our weakness whispers: Leave it to the collective, its head is bigger!

Anyhow, I shall return to the hut behind our cottage, to the hut where I sleep and where the sun shines on my bed in the morning, on Monday, on Tuesday, on Wednesday, on Thursday, on Friday and on Saturday, in short, all through the week, especially on Sunday; I shall take the rucksack, the axe and the urn, and I shall go. No, not today, today I couldn't span the horizon with my staff, for that one must make an early start ... and so I have been postponing the day for several years now. Sometimes I am not sure whether I still have the determination to do what I have to do. Of course, I could do it any day, but that would be the end of the matter, I would have to set about curing myself and I would lose the bliss that comes when pain recedes from the point of torment. Also I am not sure whether, now, it might not turn out to be no more than an empty gesture. For the moment has passed when I could have acted in the fullness of sorrow and anger, that is, with sublime right. Having subjected my idea to reason so many times since then, I fear that the sublime right of sorrow and anger may turn out to be a dead letter.

When I got home, my brother-in-law was up and in the garden, sickle in hand, cutting grass under the apple trees for the rabbits.

This peaceable man – who has earned my admiring pity for the way he has shared our family destiny, moved to a strange neighbourhood, changed his trade, attended evening classes and risen to be a foreman at the works, all for the sake of winning my sister, three children, this cottage and a tranquil face reflecting his good heart – this brother-in-law of mine laughed and said:

"Well, has he gone?"

"Yes," I replied.

"And Karel – you've had a word with him?"

"No, I haven't seen him."

He drew the whetstone along the edge of the blade, and carried on cutting the grass. I went into Dad's hut, where I sleep and where dust holds sway over the books. When Juranda's daughter Daniela heard a scythe being hammered in the field, it was a sign for Zbyshek that his maiden was soon to die, and that is the mournful ending of a stirring tale, an ending which I could never get over. And today, if you please, of the entire story only the gist, the true essence remains with me: the dense forest, the hair of the Polish maidens. And Dad also has a cheap edition of Meyrink here, and other incredible things causing one to marvel at a spirit capable of breakfasting on anything, from works of philosophy to the most sterile trash. A spirit newly built and raw, waiting for a settled occupation to add the finishing touches, and since this never happened, the unsecured windows and doors admitted every stray breath from the prairies of the written word. Only the first generation reads in this manner, held spellbound, as he was.

Our winter Sunday mornings were as follows: the previous evening Dad would arrive back home, he would wash himself in water heated on the stove, change and make the rounds of the cottage. He would throw himself into sawing and chopping wood, into cleaning out the goat shed, pig sty and rabbit hutches, he would do three to five other things, and his overcoat on the coatstand would be holding a store of chocolate to be doled out to us in bits, and he would pet Mother, eat the choice dishes she had prepared and, at the last moment, with a glance in our direction he would let us have a morsel, then he would read, which displeased Mother, but when they went to bed he would read again until, when they had turned out the lamp, they would mumble in bed and we would hear the word problem, broblem, br, br. Next morning Mother made rye coffee in the kitchen, set the cake on the table, while Dad read in bed – *West of the Rio Grande*, *The Church of Rome Unfrocked* and, indeed, *Mein Kampf*. Meanwhile folk from Tarandova were filing past our fence on their way to church.

"Get up, the boys'll be here," Mother would call out three times, which meant that our cousins from Tarandova were coming, two or perhaps three of them, according to how many were out of work, idling the winter away at home. With the devout flock they trod the road to church, but at the moment when they should have been inside, they turned tail and made for our place, then, as the flock returned from Mass, they would fall in to walk home devoutly in their dark suits, telling each other – that's once more we haven't been in church, which was how it was almost every Sunday morning in wintertime. It should be added that Mother was sometimes upset about the sin we were taking upon ourselves, so she would have a shot at sending them away. Dad, however, would intervene: "Don't be so straitlaced!" The boys would laugh, the eldest lustily, the second in a feeble sort of squeak, while the youngest wrinkled his brow and objected in all seriousness: "What are you saying, Uncle? Aunt isn't straitlaced at all!" Whereupon all of them, Dad included, burst out in such a mighty and many-layered gust of merriment that the stove blazed up and the kitchen became unbearably hot. Of course, I never quite knew what it was all about, but I felt the bliss which always possessed me during these ritualistic visits, and so it was every Sunday morning in wintertime.

From a summer Sunday morning I retain no more than the memory of a memory, a grey path along which I stumble because I cannot distinguish the bumps very well, or am I, for God's sake, so small? The evening before Dad had said he would be going in the morning to gather the edible toadstools known as ceps. He used to go quite often, though the yield was never any match for the scale of his expeditions, indeed, any old lady popping out between milkings to the edge of the woods would collect more toadstools, therefore it is my belief that Dad's excursions served primarily to satisfy his longing to range on and on towards fresh waves of woodland, maybe without thought of the ceps, but to spend the day in silence and fasting. He was no churchgoer, but he had an instinctive need for the sublimity and the choir, and where should he find them? I long for our hills, which do not kill, the woods welcome a man, the trees nod their heads and sigh, you are safe even at night in our woods – I would almost be tempted to maintain that his forest worship derived from the romanticism of our national revival, had he not been a carpenter who also wielded his broad-axe to square that forest timber.

I had taken it into my head to say I wanted to go with him. Mother had been against. We went to bed, I was fast asleep when somehow words began to obtrude into my unconsciousness, words demanding to be understood. Limply I tried at first to ward them off, but they mumbled stubbornly on and I began to understand.

"Son, shall we go to the hills together?"

Again the words droned their warm whispering, not commanding, leaving to me whether I would break the web of lassitude to reach them. The room was utterly dark. I shivered with cold as I dressed in the clothes laid out the previous evening. I put two slices of bread and dripping in my bag.

Flat grey dawn was seeping from the earth through the barn walls, cocks crowed, dogs barked, as we walked through the village between the garden fences. Never before had I seen the street so empty, nor heard the hollow thudding of horses' hooves as they stir restlessly in their stables before dawn. Crimson was spilling over the sky from the east as we climbed the path where I was unable to distinguish the bumps very well. It was really a tangle of paths, furrowed by the torrents of spring and then smoothed over by the iron-shod wheels of beautiful waggons. Its soft dust was grey with dew. Not until we reached the first summit did we pause, and there, edging towards us from the hills, hung a strange metal disc, as heavy as a close-up star.

I no longer know the way we went, I have never succeeded in retracing the route, although always, at every turn, there has been something to remind me of it. It is really hard to tell which flanks of the beech-clad hills derive from that day and which from the folk songs of Slovakia. Merely to step over a shadowy stream in the woods has sufficed to fill me with a sudden groundless joy, or with an obscure sorrow. I hurry to reach a bare hilltop, impatiently, then I turn to race back into the valley with a feeling in my back that disaster is about to descend from up there and that at all costs I must not look behind me. There are reaches of these familiar woodlands through which, to this day, I would not venture to pass, because I tell myself that will be the last thing I have to do, before. And then there are the happy places which I have no wish to see again because I would find them terribly spoilt. With Dad, too, I always had the feeling that walking the beech woods was not simply a matter of walking to a destination, that it was a remembering through walking, and a seeking for something with his feet; he would pause so incomprehensibly above the valleys, turn back so inexplicably, jerkily cover our tracks when we had mistaken our approach to a clearing or a lumber site, and he would scan the prostrate trunks, sometimes even measuring them with his footrule, although there could never have been any question of our carrying them off. We travelled the bare ridges, where peasant axes in centuries past had hewn away the woods, setting our course as straight and surely as along lines of communication. Only at one open spot, where the crest of a fir-clad hill towers to divide the cool and the warm winds, did Dad halt, saying:

26

"Here is the place, son, you see?"

Or, a few years later:

"This place, my boy, remember it."

Only long after did I understand.

On that day, which I reproduce for myself as little more than the memory of a memory, in a valley beyond the skyline, I was suddenly taken ill. Dad tried at first to urge me on. I must say I would never venture to urge a child of mine the way he did. He said:

"Looby-looby, looby-looby, homealong . . ."

Later he carried me on his back. As it swayed to the rhythm of the striding feet, that sweat-soaked head must surely have been thinking about something to do with that time. And yet, what was to come in the world, in our parts too, thirty years on, must already have been written in Kismet, and since the past, the present and the future exist with equal validity, his head was already open there beneath the hair, only no one knew it, I did not know it, and he knew it least of all.

I could not accept that this was all: a shabby, greasy grey hat, grey trousers with a few grass stains on the knees, a corduroy jacket with the Party badge on the lapel, shoes with socks tucked inside as only a man seriously intending to put them on next day would do, a faded ulster, a fragment of chocolate, a few limp cigarettes, an address book, and then, that diary! the entries running from June to the end of the year and continuing in January of the next year, as though time were some curled up, dead dog. All this they handed to me in a waterproof bag, I could not accept that these paltry things could outlive him, a man of such worth. And of the four children, I was the one to whom it fell to make the arrangements because I live in Prague, what a coincidence that it should happen right here, in Prague . . . yet now, as I write, a sober thought strikes me, it strikes me that he did it intentionally, he wanted to end it all close to his eldest, his firstborn son, and I have discovered this, his unexpected weakness, now – five years after his death!

At the funeral the meaning of all funerals was revealed to me: they are the preparation for one's own death. The clerk asked me if four o'clock in the afternoon would be convenient. I said it would. "It's a nice hour," the clerk assured me. It was. In it I grasped that I was next in the line, the first of the four. That, however, I could accept lightly, for my thoughts were with him. It seemed to me that something in the nature of a summing up of his life was required, a key to close it all. In the hour of need I would have been ready to take any man's poem, but there had to be one sentence in it: My father built a house and died.

Ever since that day I have felt that somewhere something was handed on to me, but I am not clear what it is. Although my sister got the cottage and our cousin from Tarandova came for the broad-axe, the main thing is still waiting.

What is it?

3

After all I have said so far, it looks as if it would be well to abandon the sentimental rummaging in favour of some quite practical undertaking and, let me say straight out, to go and buy a pair of inner soles for my shoes.

A steam-roller, a nice one, is busy on the road where the new houses stand. From one block of flats to another goes the postman, pushing newspapers into the letter-boxes. Yet in one of the surviving barns something greyly stirs.

"Good day," I call out to Mrs Ovesna. No reply. The rustling straw in her hands fills the ears beneath the faded scarf.

I walk the crooked street and I pass everything, the dwellings of friends and schoolmates, the church and the public weighbridge, the abandoned forge, the discontinued pear tree with its redundant wasps. Francek the bully, whose all-powerful arms dragged me behind the barns to inflict torture by tickling, ended under a tank during manœuvres, but the comrades hushed that up. Bohus jumped out of a cock-eyed new window in Ostrava because what he had lost at cards could never be won back. Lada is in India, and years ago about six of the lads moved out to the border region, among them Vincek whose mattress caught fire from a cigarette and he was suffocated. I walk the street full of people and vehicles, the street without a single friend, as though there had been a flurry of sleet.

Over the new asphalt passes a new type of traffic, which means fewer cow-pats. Our street is beginning to resemble the street of our desire. Uniform fences, matching façades, a public garden hemmed by concrete kerbstones and iron railings. A not-eye-catching error has been committed: having taken overlong in building their settlements as they would have liked them to be, people now find they are getting the kind they used to want. What is more, by their dumb devotion to planning they tie the hands of the younger generation who, while already cherishing a different image of their community, will in their turn, by the time they begin to have a say, start building what they used to want. Obviously, a superfluous generation is emerging which really ought to disappear if the world is not to be a hideous place. A generation as strong as a bull in its prime, impetuous, and horribly jealous too, because in its youth it was never given a proper chance to do anything.

People are building everywhere, staking out new fences, and as I walk around I am not at all sure that there is anything here in which I can take part. The farmers who used to chase me have got their third set of teeth and I cannot recognize them any more. People who disliked my father now fail to recognize me. Just occasionally a head is turned, eyes raised from the pump, a memory stirred by my presence. Some of the children standing by the shop think they will be getting a new teacher after the holidays.

And here, long, long ago, a carpenter built himself a house. His wife died and he was left alone with his child. He sat in his new workshop, singing to himself. They came and took him away to the madhouse, and if he has not died, he is living there to this day.

Again, because the first telling was colourless. A young man, a carpenter by trade, built himself a house. Setting quite a grand entrance on a chamfered corner, he put his display window in the main frontage. Every bit of carpentry in this house was the work of a master craftsman. The finishing at one ·side was temporary, with jutting bricks ready for an extension. At this point, however, the carpenter's wife died, leaving him with their baby boy. He abandoned the furniture he had been making for his house, and dropped everything. Since no one placed any new orders with him, he took to wandering aimlessly about his workshop. At times he would pick up a hammer to bash any piece of wood that came his way, and he would sing. He waited and waited, but no one came. Until, in the autumn, at half past seven they came, six of them. They tied up the carpenter, he struggled and shouted, but they bundled that carpenter into a car. Never again did the carpenter come home, and it is thirty-one years now. That is outrageous.

I pass the dwellings of uncles and aunts, all from my mother's side of the family. They had ensconced themselves here like swallows under the eaves, making their living half from crafts, half from their fields. Dad used to call them "the spirit of the place", and he had in mind the way they sat under the eaves, not venturing into the world or into political life. Now I imitate his faint smile, and it is at him I am smiling.

Here is the house where our Grandad lived with Grandma. The tall brown door with the peeling paint had a little window in its upper half through which Grandad would be watching the street as I came from school not meaning to call in, but call in I did when I saw that Grandad was looking at me as he surveyed the street through the little window in the tall, brown, peeling door; for children should call on the old folk, they need to do so in order that one day they may grow old properly themselves. Grandad had grey hair and a grey beard and to a ripe old age he bore himself erect, like President Masaryk. Both had spent their youthful footloose years in Vienna, but on closer view even an idiot could see that our Grandad was more of a good-hearted fellow and less of a fighter for national independence than President Masaryk. Our Grandad wore the kind of hat favoured by the Social Democrats in the old days when allegiances could still be expressed by hats. But as I look at that door today and imagine his face in the glazed rectangle, what I seem to see, hanging on that house is a portrait of our old man – the Emperor of Austria.

The door with the portrait opened to reveal the black figure of my uncle – an orphan for many a long year now. I took a seat at the table.

"You don't smoke, do you," my uncle stated, "so have a piece of bread."

My aunt, however, placed before me a big damson tart.

"And how are you all in Prague?" she asked.

"Quite well, thank you," I replied.

"Hm! The cows always gave more milk in Prague," my uncle said.

Several cousins whom I had never met before were bickering over something, while the eldest silently cradled his son on his lap.

Notwithstanding, I asked:

"And how are you?"

My aunt laughed and my uncle opened his black mouth to say:

"All right."

"We have to be well," my aunt said emphatically, tightening her head-scarf under her chin. "They took our fields, maybe you don't know that."

"No, I didn't know, but it's happening everywhere."

"Everywhere? You don't say! I thought maybe it was only like that in our parts."

She poured out some milk for me and for my uncle, who began pacing the kitchen with his mug, drinking and picking at a piece of bread.

"Hey," he turned to me, "my pliers have fallen under the bed. Get down and fetch them for me."

In a trice I was on my belly, running my hand over the bumpy boards right up to the damp wall; it smelt of plaster and mould there. As I stretched out even more, suddenly, smack, a mousetrap snapped on my fingers. In pain and sorrow I crawled from under the bed.

Uncle laughed uproariously, so much so that the old lady, God rest her soul, scolded:

"May the good Lord forgive you!"

"And why don't you join the co-operative farm?" I asked; amazing how things have changed in thirty years.

"We can't," my uncle replied. "It's made impossible for us," he fumed.

"How's that?"

"It's not voluntary," he scoffed. "Because we can't join with a good will."

He was tearing up the bread with his fingers.

"We had the trees, well you know we had them there," my aunt said, "but the fruit rotted. When we wanted to pick it, they said we were thieves. Thieves!"

She folded her thin arms over her stomach.

"Oh well, there's no need to cry about it," said the cousin with the child on his lap, a plumber by trade. "You can always buy apples."

"Fruit in the gob, the arse has a job," interjected our old Grandad, now dead and gone, "just one sloe, arse'll always blow," he laughed, blowing rudely through his pipe, which President Masaryk, as I remember him, would never have done.

I know their field below the pine wood. It is a narrow tongue wedged between the stream and the hill. Crickets live there, and as long as they are young they are brown.

"If they needed our piece to make up a big field, I wouldn't say a word," my aunt added. "But they don't need it, and they behave like this. Two years now there's been nothing but thistles there."

She folded her thin arms over her stomach.

"Don't cry, Mother, bread can be bought."

The top side is bounded by a line of stones gathered

over a hundred years. It is a haven for lizards which, on the first encounter with me, have one tail, but by the second they have grown two.

"When I lie mouldering in the clay, who will mow your grass for hay, the grass, the grass, the green grass O."

Don't cry old man, grass can be bought, lizards can be bought, stones can be bought. We Czechs have known times like this more than once in our history, and always we have come out of them wealthier and more capable of every type of buying and selling.

"And Karel, you've had a word with him?" my aunt asked.

"No, I haven't seen him," I replied.

She simply nodded, keeping some unspoken thought to herself.

Uncle was standing by the doorway, looking out of the little window and eating bread. He asked:

"How long has your dad been – gone?"

"Five years."

"Yes, who knows," his face puckered queerly as he turned towards me, "who knows whether he really thought it would be like this . . ."

I sensed that here was the last one of my good uncles.

Continuing on my way, I met a schoolmate, we called him Pambilo. One day, when we were doing the geography of Mexico, his knowledge had been scant and the teacher, in a genial mood, had asked him if he could at least give the name of the tall, broad-brimmed hat. "Pambilo," my schoolmate had replied, looking as healthy then as now.

"On holiday? On holiday?" he cried merrily as he dismounted from his bicycle.

"Well, yes," I replied.

"And the family, quite well?" he inquired again.

"Fairly well, thank you," I replied.

"And in Prague, things are all right?" His tone was more confidential now.

"All right, on the whole," I told him.

"Well, we must take things as they come, mustn't we?" he said.

We laughed.

"And in Prague, in the shops. There's more to be had there, I suppose?"

"Well, you know, the cows always give more milk in Prague," I told him.

"They could've been doing the same here long ago," he said, looking at me intently, "if we'd had more men like your dad. He was a real Bolshevik!"

"Well, the cows have quite a bit to do with it, too," I objected, "and there used to be fifteen hundred cows here, and now you've got half the number."

For a while he gazed at me in amazement. Then, with a hesitant slap of his palm on the bicycle handlebar and his eyes straying away from me, he said:

"It's difficult. There's darkness in their minds here, you know. Each to his own little patch of land. Folk can't manage to shake off that capitalist past."

"So you must push them a bit harder," I said.

"Don't worry, we do what we can," and he smiled warmly.

"I know."

"But we haven't many workers yet, the factory isn't finished. The job your dad had to get them to approve it so there'd be a living at home and people wouldn't have to go off to some goddam place, to Turkey, or where was it your dad went?"

"To Persia," I replied.

"That's it, Persia. Well now, I'll be off." He slapped the handlebars, then, remembering something, he asked:

"And Karel – you've had a word with him?"

"No, I haven't seen him," I said.

There was a queer pause, then he slapped the handlebars once more.

"Well now, I'll be off," he laughed. "We'll put things

35

to rights, all in good time!" concluded Pambilo in the voice of a district official, which is what he is.

What may happen is that one day I shall pack up the Persian letters and send them off from the old post office here to the place whence they came. There in the wastelands they will fall to dust beneath the rugged cliffs. And there let the researchers seek them, if any of them are seriously interested in what it means for the movement when the gentry here take to drink in order to forget. Since there is no beer to be had, there is no fear of that happening to me. The hotter it is in the daytime, the colder it is at night. Sleep being impossible, one is forced to think. What about? About debts (the rain never falls on them), about decaying teeth (which plague you), about the children who are growing up or being born (and are always troublesome), about money (that most of all) and, finally, there are the dreams about a sister-in-law who is anaemic, and when one is intending to marry her one discovers she has consumption, and one forsakes her for another who, when one wants to marry her, turns out to be one's own wife whom one truly loves, and the lustful yearnings are satisfied – and really, the things one dreams about. I am trying to find the way between a man of sound mind and a madman. Some of our lads here brought it off best. Being in some hotel where there were women, too, they got into an argument with an officer, there was a fight, they broke his sword, they threw out about a hundred people, they smashed everything (people get excitable here) and they are still in gaol, and the firm has to pay 1,000 Real for each of them, which won't help anyhow, they will be deported as undesirable aliens which gives all of us a bad name. I drink, as follows: three bottles of wine a week and every morning a dram of vodka (Russian spirits), I dilute the wine with soda water. On the site, during the day, I drink tea and whatever there is to drink, even water from a bricklayer's trowel to wet my throat. I got the shits too, but that was in the beginning before I started on the vodka, which they advised me to take regularly. As to whether I am well, don't worry, I am well, and the Persians say I'm a real devil, but I am simply repaying them for the kindness they show us, but that belongs to Iran and not in a letter.

In the meantime, however, in the meantime I am conducting my researches in my own rough and ready way. The professional scholars do not strike me as being reliable. I am just as capable as they are of bending the facts to my own ends, which I do, and why? Probably I am moved by the same motive as my black-mouthed uncle – a feeling that, after all, someone has to lean hard over on the opposite side to keep the boat on an even keel.

The sweetish smell of malt wafted over the brewery wall as I bought my inner soles for two crowns; the week's meat ration for the village was being delivered to the butcher's across the road and people were queuing up. As I left the shop, I saw a flock of geese scuttling over the bridge, two chimes ding-donged from the tower, a couple of women were standing outside the tobacconist's, one was displaying a pair of kid's tights to the other, and I stood amazed at the incredible simplicity of the setting compared with the rotary press.

Am I a stranger, or do I belong? I come here as if it were home, but perhaps that is merely my imagination. It is really no argument that, in the little house under the brewery wall, soon after I was born I took a big knife to my velvety dogs and carved them into strips composed of concentric rubber bands. Yet those awful strips still lie in that house, and there is no reason why anyone should believe me.

"Hullo there," came a sombre greeting from the gateway of the fairy-tale cottage nestling beneath the brewery's towering bulk.

"Hullo, how are things?" I replied.

"I'm breathing my last," said cousin Karel, hands in pockets, as he leant against the wall by the drainpipe.

"What?"

"I'm breathing my last, can't you see?" laughed the man without wife or children. "In that I see the fulfilment of our family's destiny."

"How's that?" I inquired of my bizarre cousin. And again I was aware of that clinging sense of shame. At any moment, a word from this cousin could be followed by another word which would bring out into the open the old story of what happened between our family and theirs. By prolonging a conversation with cousin Karel, I was risking that word being uttered, yet I was oppressed by the knowledge that once more it would not be spoken and therefore it would remain. And it was with this precarious certainty, which is mine alone now that Dad is no more, that I asked Karel what in fact was the cause of his departure from this life.

"And what did your dad die of?" he asked, speaking slowly, and he concluded: "Of his own accord."

Through the mask of ineffable sarcasm a smile of stony calm was struggling to the surface by the wall. Without attempting an answer, I looked, and I saw before me a man for whom no suitable appellations are to hand even in the central storehouses of Prague. One would have to set about extracting them from someone.

"Anyhow, come for a chat some time," my cousin added in his slow way.

I made off along the lane and then through the gardens. It struck me that it would be a fine trick of time if I were suddenly to be old and absolutely alone, I would have my local nickname, and I would go off, as I was doing then, out of the village to the stream among the grey willow trees, and there on the trampled patch carpeted with silverweed would stand a poorhouse. I would breathe the scent of camomile as I walked around that poorhouse. And I would know nothing at all. In a corner of a bare room I would have my bunk. And that would be that.

But time dictates otherwise! As things are, I possess so

many things that I have an inkling about all the things I might possess. And I am horrified when I add up all the things I know. There is so very much – the minimum dosage required to shatter the ignorant bliss of a being who knows nothing. In other words, for a handful of silver the poorhouse is lost to me. And I shall grow old, nonetheless.

Coming to the stream, I saw that Pukysh the basket-maker must have died long ago. His wooden house, stacked all around with firewood and tools, had vanished from its site by the weir, and the weir itself had been levelled by the current. Probably the bed of the stream had subsided. The stream flows, but where's the fish? The cat has eaten it up. Where's the cat? She's strayed into the wood. Where's the wood? Burnt to ashes. Where are the ashes? The stream has washed them away. Where's the stream? The oxen have drunk it up. Where are the oxen? If only I knew!

Always quietly parting the curtained willows, Mrs Pukyshova would cut the osiers and lay them in her pannier. Among us boys Bohus Cimbalek was the best at catching fish. Usually he caught them under his splayed foot. The big fish in the pools are driven with a club into a basket. On Whit Sunday into the water half-way, after Trinity go in bravely. Sitting in front of his house, Mr Pukysh might have been in the Klondyke, except that he was quietly and peaceably weaving a basket. When we were all in the water, some smart lad would creep on to the bank, shouting:

> *Scrammery, scrammery, scram,*
> *Fleas in a jam,*
> *The one who scrams last*
> *Has got the fleas fast.*

And he was the one who scrammed out of the pool last. One Christmas at the time of the Nazi Protectorate, a German soldier standing guard by our tunnel asked me to catch some fish for him, because, so he said, he had an aquarium at home. His wish pleased me, but to catch a couple of minnows and sticklebacks in the stream before Christmas was a job for three days. How dreary a stream is in wintertime! Empty gurgling, ice-brittle alders, dark sky, and not a friend in sight. They are sitting around somewhere, playing halma, while they dig into a pot of dumplings sprinkled with poppy-seed. I cannot say that I have always had enough friends, for there have been times when I have felt I was walking up and down a street with not a living soul in sight, as though a flurry of sleet had passed that way.

In summer, though, the heat of the stream's bed, as white as the Rio Grande! Every summertime the naked water rolls over on a different side, leaving a plain of stones beside it for us to lie upon and the warm breeze wafts the scent of sage. Whistling Dan, how's your dog doing now?

4

The sun is shining on my bed, somebody's doves are cooing, today I shall let the letters lie, slightly yellowing they are by now, and I shall really set out. In the days of their rhythmic arrivals, confirming the theory that I still had a father, they were incomprehensible to me and I entirely failed to appreciate their connection with the way my mother's steps and movements went. For me they brought exotic postage stamps and the uplifting knowledge that my father was party to a travelogue. What, in comparison, was the miserable potato-digging to which my mother was a party! He who has no other skill digs potatoes. True, in the course of time my image of a pungently-scented dad was replaced by a vision of an avenging fate bound inexorably to return one day, and should this being prove unkind to me, it would be Mother's fault. I never liked to see her yellow brooding penmanship by the light of the oil lamp. The letters covered four pages, and I imagined them to be all about naughty children. Almost thirty years later I learn with surprise that they were not.

"Last year we cracked nuts in bed all through Christmas, you cracked them and I ate the kernels," the wife recalls, then she seals the memory and sends it on its fortnight's journey, only to read, a week later, the incomprehensible reply:

"You complain that we get nothing out of this. I would never bring home those 800 crowns a month wherever I might be in our country. That stands to reason."

The wife replies immediately:

41

"I have bought a table, you wrote back that it is no use to you."

And she is desperately sorry when she reads, a few days later:

"As long as you do not become reconciled to the idea that I am away, I shall live. Who, dear wife, will do the mowing for you?"

And so the disjointed, undeserved dialogue continues, as true as married life.

"Though I do not like having to write it, you force me to do so; what use to me is a dim memory."

"When I was afraid, you laughed at me. What horrible kind of sickness is this malaria? Dear boy, where does it actually hurt you?"

My heart is heavy today as I read their correspondence, and really there is no need to read it, I have known about it for years, so why do I poke now into these packets which, in their lifetime, were strictly taboo and remained sacrosanct long after they were dead? Little by little an invisible something has shifted to reveal them, until suddenly they have appeared in this wide world like a phantom cry from lips that died as it was uttered, while even the listening ear has died meanwhile. So now the letters once belonging to parental authority have been transformed for me into the letters of a man and a woman with whom I can be on an equal footing, all the more so, probably, because this year I am three years older than her and one year older than him, and with a better understanding because ... well, by now I have some inkling of the way I may be paid back in the same coin through my own children.

And I have reached the firm conclusion that this legacy was intended for me. To refuse it would be to neglect a last wish which, had it been consciously conceived, would have been voiced, and to do that would be tantamount to rejecting the messenger across the great divide and to courting death in the ditch.

What I meant to say, however, was that the sun was shining, the doves were cooing, and therefore I went out. At the gate I had to make a rapid choice, to turn right or left. In both cases I would have to cover some distance past other people's windows, and I was so keenly aware of my time-honoured right to scamper through the gateway barefoot and in running shorts that I was thoroughly ashamed to be parading in front of strangers barefoot and in running shorts, consequently, it was a relief to know that in reality I was quite soberly clad. All this futile manipulation of the spirit really produces nothing but a sense of defeat; beneath its weight I cringe invisibly, and all those windows can see that it is so.

How ridiculous it is of me to cling to the idea of belonging to this place – nobody is going to rob me of it, in any case, because all the newcomers here are equal in being strangers to each other, and still I persist in asserting that I belong, so much so that I begin to suspect I may be a bit wanting. Early this morning it was borne in on me very forcibly that someone else feels entirely at home here. Coming out of the hut behind our cottage (in running shorts and barefoot), I saw a figure opening a window on the first floor of the block opposite. The curtain had caught on the corner of the window, so it had to reach out to free it, which brought its breasts up into the yellow morning light, where they swayed for a while. Because I was slow in the uptake, by the time I had shifted my gaze lower I glimpsed, only for a second, above the window frame the familiar black triangle of its crotch, looking as matter-of-fact and self-assured as though no barn had ever, in times past, been standing on this spot. Well, now we in Prague are not the only people who sleep naked, I said to myself, and minded my own business.

In my pocket I carried four apples, on my back a rucksack and from the station old Mrs Ovesna was pulling a handcart loaded with firewood. She is thinking what a big shot I have become, and I am not sure whether I have or not, because the big shots keep shifting further and further away from us, until in the end those at the top must find a dreadful emptiness gaping over their heads, and that is perhaps this freedom. For my part, there is no need to be there, I can imagine it well enough. My salvation is the feel of warm dust under my feet, a sensation which comes back to me as surely as this reflex of mine is sure: going through the gate, I throw an eye at our window to see if I have managed to get away unnoticed; I get a kick out of that. When that happened, a diesel train always came rolling out of the tunnel that is as old as I am.

A diesel train came out of the tunnel that is as old as I am. I met an old-timer from the railway, who passed without recognizing me, although I can recall what his pleasures used to be. I met some new ladies whose gaze, uplifted as if on iron rods, topped my head by six inches, making it abundantly clear that they were not looking at me. I feel a stranger in the eyes of the old residents, and that stems from the fact that I am of no use to them, and to the factory settlers I am a peculiar local ephemeron; they live here not really knowing where they are living, but they live on, although they could just as well, indeed, in their own view even better, live in Prerov, for instance, a place which means nothing to them, and that is precisely the value they represent today for people who are devoted to Prerov. And I know that if I were to stand up on the hilltop, I would see an enormous school, and in each classroom a young teacher who, should anyone inquire: when will the children be putting on a play? will stare dumbly because she doesn't know, she doesn't know, she is merely earning her living, she has been appointed here, to the old people she has nothing to say, she is afraid to go to church, she has no idea on what geological formation our village lies, she doesn't know that, she simply teaches whatever knowledge she possesses, she does not sing.

I branched off from the road towards the stream, jumped over it and plunged into the willows, but a boy from the apartment block had arrived before me. Well, let's see, I said to myself.

"Scrammery, scrammery, scram, fleas in a jam – how does it go on, son?"

He looked at me in surprise, water dripped from his hand into the stream.

"I don't know," he replied.

"Fathead," I said, then I set off upstream.

The air was sweet with the scent of soapwort and I began to suspect I had been unfair to the boy. He was no fathead, he was merely the son of a fathead. The soapwort still scented the air, its virgin fragrance as pure as white linen travelled the smooth-washed stones and wove through the supple osiers in a benevolence which by degrees, from backwater to backwater, enticed me to admit that he was not even the child of a fathead but the child of one in bondage to fatheads, that was it, and the hills which filter the scant water through three old villages must see how it is, for it is as clear as daylight that he who fails to merge with the spirit of the place will also never devote his thought to it, he will not win or hold it for himself, all he will do will be to destroy everything in fury, and anyhow he will perish of hunger. Yet the day will come when the water has cleansed itself of the putrefaction of his flesh and above the stench the soapwort will rise triumphant, its virgin fragrance travelling the stones, mingling with the water, and in that water, a fish. But the further I advance against the current, the further from the filth, the more benevolently I seem to be inclined, and it must be due to those breasts this morning!

Only now has it occurred to me to wonder where that German can have hailed from; he must have come from Bremen, from a region with different fish.

When the Germans trooped into our streets, having no friends, because there was sleet, Dad was in the kitchen making a shoe-scraper. The floor was littered with shavings, Mother said:

"So now our capital will be Berlin?"

"Goose," said Dad, spitting thinly into the shavings and Mother ducked her head, for the disapproval meant for Berlin had landed on her.

A year later, in March, the noticeboard installed by the Germans next to the post office bore a photograph of our late President Masaryk in profile, bearing the following caption inscribed in German: *Half-breed Masaryk. He cannot disguise his Jewish extraction.*

Burning to know what kind things the notice-writers had to say on the occasion of the great man's birthday, I stood there until I had the sentence by heart. Then I trotted home and wrote it down at once, before searching the dictionary.

"Scoundrels," said Dad, having heard the translation.

"But he's dead, anyhow," said Mother by the stove.

Five years later, when the front had edged to Ostrava and to southern Moravia, German artillery arrived and started to dig in on the level ground around our village. People left their homes to take refuge in the woods and upland meadows, in haysheds and summer byres. Almost overnight the inhabitants of several German houses – excise men and their families – vanished from our district. Our Dad caused some surprise by conducting his brood to the entry of our tunnel, the trains having stopped running through it the previous week. There we seated ourselves on a rug and stayed put. It was mild. Two Germans mounted the ridge of the tunnel, tommy-guns in hand, on their backs drums of coiled cables; they were laying a line from the guns to some hill or other. That was before lunch, when it was time to milk the goats. Mother left the tunnel to go and milk the goats, and by the time she had returned with the milk, our good Germans were winding up their cable again, emitting a sound as melodious as a tangled roll of wire.

"Run and ask them," Dad said.

"Don't send the boy to them" said Mother.

I went up to them, the soles of their jackboots were sliding on the steep, damp slope.

"Please, why are you doing something different now?" *fragte ich*, that is to say, I asked them in German.

They were nervously jerking the cable off the branches of an apple tree and angrily slinging their tommy-guns across their chests with the air of men who, when climbing a mountain in the heat of the day, have realized that they have saddled themselves with a superfluous piece of baggage. They were young. Then one of them answered:

"The devil's taken Hitler!"

The pungency of this news even pierced the armour-plating separating his German from the German I possessed. Dad was excited in silence, Mother said:

"If only there isn't that unemployment again!"

Barely had the Germans dragged their guns from the fields and gone away, than a state of manifest anarchy set in. It is a sight to be seen very rarely – people left for a while without government. For about six hours everything carries on as usual – from force of habit, decency, shame, from the stores laid in. But as evening draws in, the wretches make their appearance here and there around the backyards. They have horses, a waggon, they are out to loot. They load up cupboards, feather beds and pianos, books they turn on to the floor and they haul the bookcases into their cellars where they pack them with jars of lard, whereupon they are ready to accept any proclamation, even, say, of a people's republic. Of course, the others are indignant at these goings on, some of them visit the deserted houses to ascertain the extent of the damage, and while there they take away a few trifles because those others might steal them, although they should have had enough already. Less and less remains in the houses, consequently the group excursions which now go just to have a look, enter by the front doors, chatter loudly and

47

serve each other as witnesses that there was nothing left anyhow. Mother brought back a ladle from an excursion, it had been lying on the steps and someone might have trodden on it. Whoever, after two days, had not been in one of these houses was undoubtedly intending, at a more suitable time, to parade his honesty in the market place! – pressure like that can be withstood only by characters of granite, who go their way regardless. When I entered, I found the floor littered with books. Some were marked by footprints. I began the futile job of piling them up a bit. Under the window lay the drawer of a bedside table, which some farmer would be missing. Suppressing a prudent squeamishness, I burrowed with two fingers among letters, coupons and family photographs, until at the bottom I reached my booty, something which I knew about purely from hearsay and reading, a packet of french letters. Dad did not go looting.

In the end, however, the honour of the village was saved when the last, unexpected enemy column, left with the job of blowing up the bridges (how could we idiots have thought they would simply go away!), was passing through, and several unarmed citizens attempted by dint of ostentatious crawling to divert the enemy from their main target, and in the process a young man was killed. However, the bridge was saved, but by an ordinary shotgun.

The road was open for the tanks of salvation, but in their place, accompanied by the short-paced trotting of little horses, came rolling in a column of farm waggons loaded partly with hay, partly with something else, and the men sitting on top were mild, elderly and voluble Taras Bulbas.[1] Any fear that the enemy might return was now dispelled, for the roads were jammed tight with Tarases. About six of them stayed a night with us. Scouting round the cottage, examining everything with cautious eyes, they

[1] Taras Bulba, folk hero of Gogol's epic of the same name, was a leader of the Ukrainian Cossacks against the Poles in the sixteenth century.

converse quietly together, then the highest-ranking, a lance-corporal with a moustache like the handlebars of a bicycle, asks Dad:

"Worker?"

"Yes," replies the recipient of the question in Russian, rather inadequately to my mind considering that he had been as far away as Persia. The recipient of the question explains, however, that in any case the men are Ukrainians.

But dissatisfaction at the answer is most evident among those fathers in uniform. Sitting warily sideways to the table, on the ottoman and on their packs on the floor, they regard the stove, the electric-light bulb hanging from the ceiling, the brass window fastenings, Mother's dresser acquired, actually, during the Hitler occupation, they mutter together, rubbing thick-veined hands, until another, young and more incisive, takes up the matter anew:

"You worker?" he repeats.

"Yes, yes," Dad repeats likewise.

And words pass round the circle; there's no help for it, he insists he is a worker, it beats me – of course, the words go round the circle in Ukrainian.

"Your house?" inquires Lance-Corporal Bulba once more.

Dad sees his opportunity, he goes to the door, claps his hand on the frame and says, in a mixture of Russian and Czech:

"My house! That I made myself!"

Six pairs of eyes are turned to that hand clamped to the door frame. I look at it too.

He felled the trees, he hewed them into beams. He staked out and started digging the foundations, but for the most part Mother had to finish the job. Sometimes she would take me with her, but I was content on that clayey field only on the condition that I could find a hedgehog, and I ask you, how many times can that happen in half a

49

day. Bricks, stone and sand were hauled by cows under the direction of the black-mouthed uncle. And our cousins helped with the building. Money and more money was lent by the savings bank, by Grandad, godfather and in-laws. Delving among all those bills today, it strikes me as incredible that two hard-working people had to pay off these relatively insignificant sums over so many years that in the end the interest had almost outstripped the money they had borrowed.

And when the supreme act of construction was about to be accomplished, came the discovery that the tie-beams and rafters had vanished. A deep track ran through the grass, to be lost on the muddy path in a tangle of other prints. They were not the only ones with horses and a cart!

The great majority of you are not carpenters, but those of you who are know that carpentry is a job where you proceed with your chisel at a speed of inches along an indistinct line leading down the tree trunk, you keep your blue eyes lowered like a plumb line to ensure that a vertical plane shall be truly vertical, and through all those hours of carpentering you have the house thought out down to the last peg. In your mind's eye there are even sides of bacon hanging on their beam, in your mind's eye the house may even burn down before it is completed, it happens both ways. Unquestionably, however, you are capable of facing all the difficulties and the risks if, right from the moment when the first splinter flies from the tree trunk, you can see before you the finished house. The vision lends meaning to everything, even to all the necessary detours, though they may lead, perhaps, to the hole in the loo. And should anyone close up this one feasible path under your nose with a tight-fitting lid, as is the custom today, your personality would surely burst in an explosion of frustration. Without the house which you can build, you cannot live; it is an outrage.

Dad was stocky, his brow was angular, his chin and cheek-bones jutting. In normal circumstances his features played softly and were full of remarks such as: "Catch hold of this, mind you don't miss." Or: "And that's that." But a series of persistently hard blows could transform that face into an immobile mask presaging an outburst of awful rage.

When the timber was lost, Dad was ten years younger than I am today. Mother sobbed herself to sleep, then woke herself with crying, while he didn't come home at all that night.

5

He returned in the grey dawn, refused to explain, hung his cap on the hook by the window, and when Mother had hastily given him something to eat, he told her, from under the peak of his cap again, not to say a word to anyone but, above all, to bring lunch for four to the site.

On the grass behind the barn lay a model of the roof, made of boards. Measuring and fitting the pairs of finished rafters on the model were – guess who – two cousins from Tarandova! Strong roof-trusses already rested firmly on the red walls, while Dad and a third cousin were busy raising the tie-beam.

She could not believe her eyes nor grasp what was happening. She called out, but they gave no answer, and goodness knows why they didn't. They made a show of whistling and shouting to each other.

"Up she comes! And up! Hey-ho!"

The heavy beam knocked chips off the brickwork.

"Uncle, to me!"

"Cant her, now!"

Going to the other two by the model, she questioned them.

"Good day to you, Aunt! Ask no questions and you'll be told no lies," the younger said, and at these words an awful suspicion assailed her.

"Put in your thumb, and your hand will be in the goulash!" the elder admonished, and with a sharp tug at the handsaw he compelled his brother to give his mind to the job.

Then they marked up the timber, then they trimmed

it, their lips innocently curved and the pencils sitting very firmly behind their ears.

"Come now," said the elder after a while, addressing his aunt, "let's look at it like reasonable people; you had your timber ready, yesterday it was here. So today, you see, we are making the rafters from it. What goodies have you brought us?" and he burrowed in her bag, uncovering the pan of food.

With a scared glance around, she said:

"Well yes, but somebody stole it from us!"

The younger cousin, who had by now also grasped the peculiar make-up of the truth about timber, exclaimed:

"Goodness, the whole world's a den of thieves these days!"

Dad and the eldest cousin clambered down from the rooftop, it was lunchtime. They all sat on planks, eating with noisy relish, and sawdust from their eyebrows fell into their soup. These three nephews were more like Dad's brothers, an impression increased, for instance, when waving his spoon above his head, Dad started singing in Slovak: "*They went forth and round about, hunting there but finding nowt,*" whereupon all three raised their spoons and joined in: "*Heifer in a barrel, water flowing o'er her,*" which is, of course, an insignificant detail, but having heard the song many times since, I have taken note that just as mountains recede in waves and each wave in turn is less familiar, so waves of language recede, from the known to the unknown, while somewhere in the half-known, close at hand yet far away, it acquires a new, exalted sound: losing their commonplace utility, the words assume a loftier role. Indeed you, to whom a heifer in a barrel is certainly of no interest and can be ignored, might try quietly repeating several times what came next:

They sat in judgment on me, the masters and the throng,
How could they pass their judgment, when I had done no
*   wrong.*

Mother then laid a sausage on bread for each of them, folded her hands over the empty bag and prepared to weep.

"But you've taken that wood from somewhere . . ."

Her eldest nephew silently deposited his food on a plank, stood up and set his cap firmly on his head.

"Good-bye, Uncle . . . Somebody round here seems to be hinting that I'm a thief."

She looked fearfully at him, then at her husband, who continued his meal as he said:

"Exceptional times call for exceptional deeds."

The two younger nephews looked at the eldest accusingly, as much as to say that the game should not be taken too far. And he, with a laugh, sat down again beside them on the plank. For a while they munched thoughtfully, the house standing unfinished nearby.

"Aunt," said the eldest, putting an arm round her shoulders, "you're a fine lass. You surely know that we're not the ones who did the stealing, but some horrible lout. And he must have been a big swine, because he didn't go where there's wood in plenty, he came to a poor chap. So you see, we've put right what he did when we should have been sleeping as befits hard-working Christians like us."

Thus spoke the cousin from Tarandova, and I am now following the stream towards a village where the first cottages look out from crooked gardens. Little fish dart away from my feet and I am carrying my shoes in my hands, for after all, I am approaching a place of pilgrimage and a legend. But before that I shall come to a weir, and there I end, to wade on as a little boy fifty years before my time, and although there is no question of our being able to meet, we shall be aware of each other.

Around the wooden houses go women in black and grey with white – that is the classic style of photographs and of dreams about the dead. White beans are flowering behind the palings, moss has grown over the shingles of the roof, they have shooed the hen off the table and, in the red feather-bedding, children are born, one smaller than the other, until there comes the smallest who will barely remember his mother. A pale shadow with the scent of a starched kerchief will flit across his memory, and that most frequently with the blue-soft blossoming of the cornflowers. And however hard he may cudgel his brains to give a more precise definition to his flickering vision of a woman, all that the boy will glean will be – an ear of rye on the palm of his hand.

The father, on the other hand, has quite palpably fallen asleep behind the cottage on a Sunday. He lies face downwards, he is old, wearing a white linen waistcoat and goslings are pecking at the grass around his head. When he awakens the lad will bring him his cob-pipe from the room. Then they will go together up the hill where in a season butterflies give place to voles, and over the years potatoes alternate with rye. This patch of earth, where men have delved a thousand times, is called Kopanka, and down its slope run bands of trees. Breathing painfully, the father rests against an old tree trunk, picking at the fissured bark. Bending back a twig of an apple tree, he unfolds the curled leaves to crush the greenfly. Trees are the chief inhabitants of the land. The fruit tree is man's friend, and when the grey-black bloom of autumn comes again, we shall heap the damsons in pails and make jam.

Tarandova was the first other place I ever knew. It was completely different, yet exceedingly familiar, a place where groundless joy combined with unaccountable sorrow in a different way. It was also more rudimentary in character, thereby intimating that there is such a thing as history. The cottages there more openly acknowledged their debt to the woodcutter's axe, the footbridge spanned the stream only from one flood to the next, fire was, like the cat, no more than a beast tamed, held at bay beneath the iron plates of the stove thanks purely to invocation and, chiefly, to strict vigilance.

For a long time I was unaware that the man we visited, the tall, bony chap with a sardonic smile ever present on his long lips, was Dad's eldest brother, the father of my Tarandova cousins. They might have been father and son, so great was the dissimilarity and so reponsible and dignified the relationship between them. The room was always full of people, and as to who belonged to whom I had no idea, nor can I ever hope to know. In any case, it's over and done with. I could not have altered anything. In so far as my hazy memories serve me, the conversation sounded, to my confused mind, as follows:

"Fifteen black birds we dug up when drought emptied the barns," Dad's brother said, his eyes half closed.

"Aye, she smothered him!" cried his wife, startling several people.

Dad's brother rubbed his broad chin, grimaced and remarked with a doubtful expression:

"Raw timber. For the church?"

"Forty hellers a piece," someone replied, "and their old man was struck dead by lightning at the gipsy's."

"Beyond the River Vah, silt and swamps, fill up, I'll fill yours, beyond the Vah."

Silence always followed words such as these.

"After independence?" someone asked, opening the oven to look into it.

"No, before."

"After, don't talk nonsense," the voices boomed, and they hadn't any cakes.

"Say what you like, but rye won't grow. Take it from me."

"They were small, there were four of them, but as small as your hand."

"He's going to enlist."

I tugged Dad's coat.

"What birds, what black birds?" I wanted to know, but in vain. Either it was not for young ears, or for the rest of my life I have misheard.

Were I to try today to convey the impression left by that hollow where water oozed from every bank, bees flew out from the logs beneath the linden tree and in clay milk-pans the cream rose quietly to the top, I would be turning the pages of an old Czech school reader about the journey to school . . .

Along that road the elder brother carried the younger on his back because snow had fallen and they had only one pair of shoes between them, which in no way deterred that barefoot, yet bright, lad from reciting to us forty years later this verse:

Oxen
Drawing the load with plodding gait they go,
And seldom does the carter's "hey" resound,
Wisdom itself from those great eyes doth flow,
Sublimely calm, beneath the yoke resigned.

Of what followed he recalled no more than disjointed snatches, and sometimes, behind his brow, that brother was marching to the Great War, where presenting himself at the rendezvous with the enemy, he was cut down by the first shot. The poem must have held some mournful cipher for Dad, because I actually discovered among his last notes from the Party school this fragment written on a piece of pink blotting paper:

And plodding oxen draw the heavy load,
model of slavedom, abasement of the brute . . .

On making this discovery on the blotting paper, my head recoiled as though under a sharp, invisible lash from something I had not heeded nor taken into account any more. Or had I forgotten the Barefoot Boy? Can I have forgotten him?

To tell the truth, I took off my trousers and waded into the water. Because I had reached the weir. The water was not roaring, merely frothing, with yellowish foam swirling in the corners like an old man's mouth. With my hands I swept the foam away and from the bottom I fished up a rotting boot which I hurled into the willows, whereupon things were much better. Collecting a few biggish stones, I dammed the outflow, packed muddy sand around, causing the water to rise, and things were even better. Only I'm too much alone, it occurred to me, and that is not really what I'm after. Not that I try to avoid people – it is just that I look for moments which few people are looking for today, and my solitude is a by-product of this. But what can I do about it? I won't go there. And yet the greatest, the joy of joys would be if now, above the weir, I were to see Tonda from the little house in the shadow of the Tarandova mansion, Tonda the erstwhile faithful maintenance man of the weir, who used to fish out old boots and build dams to raise the water level. When he had raised it sufficiently, he would cry out to all and sundry:

"Tatra photos, hold it!"

And ducking right under, he would hoist into view the split contour of his bare bottom. And things would be much, much better.

At school Tonda counted as an awful rascal, but below the surface he was a very weepy rascal who took everything very much to heart. His sense of honour was of the first order, I know that. Our cottage was the last in the village and theirs was the first in Tarandova, so that we were, in fact, neighbours, with two miles of excellent waterway between us. He had three goats which engaged my attention right from our first acquaintance, because they were so extraordinarily restive compared to other goats, and I couldn't think why Tonda didn't tie them to a tree and wallop them with the rope. Really they gave him some bad moments. I gaped with surprise, too, the first time I visited their home; there was hardly any furniture, just battered ruins infested by a wild swarm of Tonda's brothers and sisters, while their frail mother was out in the fields and their dad was in the woods. And it is autumn, a ground mist is drifting over the heads of cabbage, the mood is one of hopeless melancholy. Words cannot tell how wonderful at such times is the sudden whistle of an approaching friend. We stood together, Tonda and I, in the cabbage mist above the black pool topped with scummy foam, in his pocket we had some matches and at intervals we threw an old boot into the water.

One day, also in autumn, when a misty afternoon twilight was hanging over the empty fields, Tonda put on his uniform and said:

"If you don't hand it over, madam, we shall be obliged to lock you up."

Dazed with shock, she retreated from the gate. Two official buyers of agricultural produce stepped into the yard, the man from the district stood hesitantly in the middle, the local man advanced towards the cellar door, when from the shed nearby the farmer rushed out waving an axe, screaming in frenzy:

"I'll kill! Another step, and I'll kill!"

Instantly, the village withdrew into the backyards, and nobody wanted to watch or see. And the animal which detested the touch of a strange hand, now driven into the furthermost corner, withdrew in horror into itself, exposing its quivering entrails. One thrust there was enough to put it out of its misery. In the newspapers they could write: SUFFERING GROWS EVER LESS IN OUR LAND.

Next day seven people who owned a few acres were dismissed from the factory in order to bring home to them that it is from mother earth, not from industry, that we draw our nourishment. Five plastic loudspeakers blared over the Tarandova rooftops. First they played a gay song, then from the stock of subjugated citizens they picked ten or so who were summoned to the Council office, where at midday the proposal was laid before them that they enter upon their happy future; having with one voice refused the offer, the said citizens went home by dark. The loudspeakers conferred for a long time and found that they had made a mistake. Next morning they commenced inviting people one by one, announcing that whoever failed to put in an appearance would be liable to a fine of twenty crowns. Most of those invited came, always at two-hour intervals, again and again, as the loudspeakers decreed. This, however, prevented them from carting manure to their fields. Only a few did cart manure and they, on hearing their names announced at two-hour intervals from the loudspeakers, muttered each time: "Another twenty, that'll make sixty now." By the second day, however, they lost count; turning deaf ears to the loudspeakers, they set to ploughing, during which some of them audibly broke wind. In their simple manner they were declaring thereby that, after all, it is from mother earth, not from the loudspeakers, that we draw our nourishment.

I was moved by this tenacity, and I wondered whether it served any purpose. It does not, that has been taken from it. But it has a value. A value that it would be well to cherish for the eventuality of the Germans coming. Perhaps that can be managed, because the buyers are only after potatoes. As long as they get the potatoes, and all that the regulations require, there can remain in all of us anything, anything, absolutely anything.

"A most interesting angle," the chief said, "only we would get nowhere by publishing it." With these words he returned my article.

"It's not a matter of getting anywhere," I said, "but merely of bawling, at least!" But I made for the door just the same. After all, I know how things stand as well as he does.

"All right, all right. Your honest soul can bawl, but the paper will be bawled out, and we'll go with it," the chief retorted amiably and automatically.

The staff trainee remarked in an undertone:

"And so we're well on the way to becoming prostitutes . . ."

The chief lifted his hands wearily; he had no desire to go on repeating the same words, but what could he do:

"If we allow ourselves to be thrown out, our places will be taken by even worse prostitutes. So what's the use?"

Following this agreed formula, it was Slavek's turn to do his comic act:

"Correct. In our hands lies the decision about the degree of prostitution that this small nation can permit itself."

We laughed.

And when the fines in Tarandova had run into thousands, an old man, his name was Horak, said he would go to the town hall and tell them something. He was as good as his word. When he entered the office, there were about ten people present: three from the Council, one representing the railwaymen of the far-away railroad, two from the Red Cross, somebody from the Party, and the prosecutor (representing the trade-union branch of employees at the district law courts). Somewhat in the corner, beside an art nouveau safe, stood my childhood friend Tonda, his split bottom meticulously concealed beneath his uniform. Horak said:

"Well now, you've made debtors of us, and since we won't pay you anything, I can see you making parasites and thieves of us, too. But if any of you gentlemen can give me his word that in the lock-up you'll at least stop jabbering at us, then I tell you straight, better there than in freedom like this!"

Turning to the corner, he held out his crossed hands, saying:

"Tonda, lock up."

For a while they looked each other in the eye, until Tonda could stand it no longer, he dropped his eyes and applied for transfer to Bohemia.

September and October, in Tarandova those were always the months for making damson jam and laying down for *slivovitz*; they also dried Wenceslas pears. This was usually the time for one of our periodic visits. Voices boomed in the room, on Kopanka the last damsons were hanging in heavy grey drops from the black branches and in the drying room the young people laughed as they turned the handle of the vat. The year when Dad was in Persia I ran off as usual to Tarandova, alone for the first time. Actually I was drawn there by a longing for loud voices, although I didn't realize that. It was enough to make you weep. As though I was among strangers. Of course, nothing worse had really happened than that among a dozen brats nobody, quite naturally, noticed my presence. I was an utterly insignificant figure; I alone attributed some kind of significance to myself and therefore I sent a complaint to Persia. The reply was as follows:

Shakhabdullazim 16/X 1936

My dear son!

Accept my warmest greetings from the land of eternal summer and eternal ice, from the land of Turkish soldiers and ships of the desert. Here they do not make damson jam and with regard to your not having the shits during the jam-making, that is a pity. They must have made it badly there. But never mind, I have sh-t here enough for the whole family. My boy, they gave you nothing and you think it was because I was not with you? You may be right, but it is rather a sharp judgment on your part. First, there is the question whether they invited you. I have no wish to sow mistrust in your heart. They may perhaps think that if your dad is in Persia he will never come back again and the bond of kinship will not count any more. However, you are no better. You think that if your dad is not at home you need not obey, and it is the same all round. And then, instead of filthy you write fillthy. Aint is incorrect, am not is correct. They don't like him, and not he. You use common expressions. Otherwise everything seems to be in order. I wonder if you go to church? To the Sokol gym etc.? Diligence in learning (German), good behaviour, I want all that to be in perfect order. Here I have become accustomed to being obeyed, so be sure you take the necessary steps in good time. Love from Dad.

I was just walking through the kitchen, the wet snow of early spring lay outside, it occurred to me to look out of the window, and what did I see! Standing on the path, gazing into our window with a wide-mouthed laugh – Dad. I rushed into the hall and from the hall into the yard and behind me everybody, my sister and the toddler brother who is now in Slovakia, they ran in their stocking feet into the snow, while on the threshold stood Mother with our driver brother in her arms. I had no ill thoughts, not a single one of my fears entered my mind at that moment, although I had not been good, nor did I know German, and I had been skipping church more and more. The natural desire to break free was submerged at that moment by the more elemental and ancient need for the strong protective arm.

For many days and numerous weeks I was moved by the resolve to be worthy. To possess, as he did, a sufficient and enduring purpose in mind which knows well in advance what is to come and therefore what must be done to further, or alternatively, to counter the events. To possess a sufficiently vigorous will to action when unexpected or downright bad things occur. I thought that, in part, I would acquire these qualities by practice, and that it was partly a matter of physical size, that is, a matter of time. When I grew big, I would be good and resolute. Time passed, but I observed no special virtues in myself, on the contrary, I noticed that as I shed the sins of childhood I was acquiring others more suited to a grown man. Indeed, in recent years I have been possessed by the fear that my decline may have started before I ever attained my highest point. A man should definitely do the best thing in his life at the moment when the balance between his good and bad qualities is at its optimal point. But who is to judge of that? To judge the moment and also to hit upon the deed to be done? The trouble is that by the time the necessary discrimination has arrived, the resolve to devote oneself heart and soul to a noble purpose is fast waning and romantic altruism has given way to a mature sense of economy.

To return, however, to the jam-making in Tarandova, which is the real issue. On that occasion they gave me not even a lick, and twenty years later the whole village was awaiting the trial of the gaffer who had raised his axe against a public official. Several farmers who were made of less strong stuff had, by then, wearily acquiesced in having a happy future at an earlier date than was possible at the normal pace of tardy, yet perhaps more lastingly, happier futures. Actually, these husbandmen will deliver to society children of inferior quality – with a gene of submission. To think that the government has not yet tumbled to that! The other farmers maintained their resistance but, in error, they cleaved to the Bible, seeking there the words to fit their case. One very old man even wrote to the President. Two more soberly minded citizens betook themselves to the Chairman of the District Council. They would talk the matter over with him. He hailed from their village, they had minded the geese together, as the saying goes when it has a merely metaphorical validity.

"Look here, Chairman," they addressed him. "First show us prosperity where a co-operative's been set up."

They sat informally by his desk. Their two hats were hanging on the stand beside his hat. The three hats were identical, in that respect the revolution had done its work.

"But see you don't give us an example from the fat

pastures over Hana way !" one of those clever hats added hastily.

The chairman smiled, thoughtfully rubbing the stubble on his chin. For a while he was silent.

"Hm! We've no time, lads. These are exceptional times and they call for exceptional deeds," said Dad, uncompromisingly devoted to the interests of these fellow men, interests which they themselves were still unable to perceive.

How much older was he then? Ten years older than I am. And in those exceptional times which persisted in requiring exceptional deeds, and always the same deeds. Mother would frequently cry herself to sleep and wake herself again, because he was away from home all night long.

6

Not far from the weir where I am now busying myself, a farmer, or gaffer, had a meadow. Once upon a time he felled a giant oak at the upper end of this meadow. The tree laid itself so neatly among its younger neighbours that the farmer had to saw it up in order to remove the timber. Naturally, he started at the thinner end and when he had reached a thickness of over three feet, he went home, leaving that oak unheeded for five years. But we, on the contrary, took good heed of the tree.

Dad's return from Persia opened the second chapter in our lives, and very nice it looked, too. The Tarandova cousins resumed their visits, sitting there listening in their black suits to the interminable tales about Persia; the eldest would have gone there straight away had he not, correctly, feared the outbreak of war. Consequently, he got married and left Iran to the Iranians. Our lives took a normal course, and of an evening we sometimes sang. Our saw and our axes emerged from a state of bluntness into a state appropriate to our family and at the spring market Mother bought a piglet so that there would be something to slaughter for Christmas.

At times, however, Dad would come home pale, his teeth chattering so much that he could hardly speak, and when he clenched his teeth his shoulders shook. Mother would put the frail wreck to bed, piling the feather covers upon him and in the Persian basket she would hunt for the box of quinine. In the midst of one such low-spirited occasion she remarked:

"That's what you have for going there!"

"Well, I shan't be pestering you for long," he replied.

With the look of one who knows, she said:

"Hm, I'll be the first to go."

Sitting anxiously in the corner, I sensed some mysterious threat passing back and forth. My sister, whose eyes always grew big with fear, advanced to the bedside where, leaning over slightly, she said:

"Daddy, where does it hurt? In your head? Or your leg? Or your tummy?"

His smile twitched as he said:

"Children, above all beware of bed! Think how many people die in bed, and how many at a crossroads. Yet there's a policeman standing at the crossroads, but in bed there isn't."

He slept for several hours. When he opened his eyes again, he gazed vacantly at the ceiling. Then, with a sharp jerk, he turned his head towards the room, saw we were there, and jerked back; this he did over and over again, like a machine or a clown. I could see that his good humour was returning; but what I failed to see, or at least did not properly appreciate, was that Mother's attitude to all this was quietly sceptical. Pushing off the bedcovers, and adjusting his long underpants, Dad proceeded to raise his tensed legs, whereupon, like a gymnast in tights landing from the parallel bars, he executed a flying leap to the floor. Darkness was falling outside the window at the time, we had not lighted the lamp because we were playing blind man's buff. The little brother, who was then still a long way from being in Slovakia, was blindfolded because he wanted to be, Mother with the driver on her lap was sitting by the kitchen range, which through its chinks cast a flickering firelight upon the walls, and she laughed as with her knees she fended our brother off from the fire while he very craftily groped around the kitchen, but without catching anyone. He would probably be searching to this day, because Dad had hung the two of us, my sister and myself, on the coat-rack, covering us with an overcoat, but then the rack broke away from the wall with laughter, our brother pulled the handkerchief from his eyes, and from that day right up to the present complicated times whenever any of us play blind man's buff we make first of all for the coat-rack. But there is never anybody there.

Another pastime which Dad enjoyed was when he and I used to see who could push harder at the other's head. Braced against the wall and the furniture, we faced each other on all fours, shoving until our necks creaked and Mother said it was awful and she couldn't bear the sight. Then Dad would stealthily rub his crown, and so would I, he rubbed his crown, but smiled the while. You might try that – to rub your crown and smile. You will certainly succeed, you will smile, but only so long as you don't find a hole in the bone, which puts an end to all laughter.

For several days after he arrived home from Persia in March, Dad took things easy around the cottage, in the shed, and upstairs, until he had adjusted to the temperature and the food. Then he fetched his staff and we set out.

"Don't go," Mother begged.

A sprinkling of fresh snow had fallen, there was a light, healthy frost and a film of ice crunched in places beneath one's feet. As we followed the high tracks along the ridges, the villages were lost to sight in the dank smudge; the countryside seemed flattened, its grey emptiness traversed by crows continually flying up, only to settle with loud croakings a few fields on. A cold, desultory breeze swayed the wild rose sprays and the wrinkled leaves of the hornbeams rustled lifelessly. Little eddies of snow gently swept out nooks beneath the hawthorn bushes. Suddenly, Dad, who was striding ahead of me, gave a long bellow, and when I looked at him I saw he was laughing! Planting his staff in a snowdrift, he turned to face the grey east, fell upon his knees, hands raised above his head, bowing and crying:

"Allah-o akbar!"

He sent his cry in the direction where there was undoubtedly warmth and light, but where all we could see was the mournful silhouette of hills against the cold, desolate sky. He took his staff and pointed to the red skin of the bare linden twigs with buds, then to the tangled web of tracks traced by beasts of all sizes and shapes, while I, in my turn, pointed to a steep bank, bare of snow, which was riddled by an incredible number of holes of all possible calibres. Spring was on the way! I realized how terribly happy he was to be back, which somehow made me afraid and for a few seconds I was sorry for Mother who had not wanted to let us go.

We circled back into the valley, and as we were descending obliquely to the meadow at which I am now looking, we made a sudden left turn in the order of our march, because in that order we had remembered the oak, and there it was lying on the steep slope, neatly wedged among the trees, and whoever wanted to take it would have to make at least two sections. We walked around it, muttering under our breath.

"Hm, that's a teaser," Dad said, jabbing with the metalled tip of his staff at the bark, which fell away in big, curved strips.

"It's negligence of the most glaring kind," was my comment.

"Two can play that game, cried Texas Jack," Dad said.

"And in a trice the scoundrel was immersed head first in the treacherous bog," I reciprocated.

There is no point in recounting the day-long travail which we brought upon ourselves by this lofty design. It was a good half-day's work to saw once through the trunk. No one else would have attempted the job, certainly no peasant, clod-hopping, country-yokel character. Towards evening, I could pull the saw no more than three times across the trunk before pausing to rest. And it was no better when I knelt on the top and sawed beneath me, or when I changed places with Dad to brace myself under that monstrous log, my feet slithering down the slope and sawdust falling into my eyes. It must have dawned on the father that he had overrated his son, and now he was paying for it. The feat, when we had achieved it, was one more hard won victory of the spirit over vile matter, and no more than that, for our corporeal matter was enfeebled, whereas the tree remained a mighty thing. Dad was, actually, just the age I am now, and I was eleven at the time, which was the age at which he, as I knew, was already working at odd jobs, and sometimes the sister-in-law who ran the home in place of his mother wouldn't even let him go to school, and so on, as the tales of fathers always run; but what if it were really so? I wondered as I considered that log and I wonder today as I consider the log-book I am keeping, what if he really had no shoes, could never read and always had to lend a hand, sometimes hungry, too, and only now am I beginning to take it seriously, now we are the same age, when everyone has shoes and so on, but when I have to ask myself: so what? What a tragedy, what a tragedy! We all have shoes, so what? I believe that in respect of that oak tree Dad, like myself, had succumbed to the impression that his stay abroad must surely have signified a turning point in the history of our family, and as though time had been multiplied by distance, he imagined that I had grown up during our separation more than I had in reality. At last the trunk split apart for a second time.

"Bloody shitting job!" Dad sprawled on the ground, panting in Persian to avoid corrupting me.

The sweat poured down me, my legs shook, I could not close my swollen hands and all the tubes in my chest were on fire. Miserably, I said nothing, and he added indulgently:

"Striking a well-aimed blow with his fist, he stunned the scoundrel!"

But I failed to reciprocate.

We did what remained to be done: to shift the three mighty logs from their petrified bed and propel them down hill. They rolled in fantastic somersaults, earth spurted from them, they roared like the elements and caused us enormous delight.

"Halloa, a merry ride right to the gates of hell!" I reciprocated.

"Logs," was the matter-of-fact comment of little brother, who was always to be found kneeling on the table by the window to see the world go by.

"Goodness, aren't they our logs?" Mother cried weakly as she, too, looked out.

Unbelieving, but fearing the worst, I rushed to the window, and I saw a waggon rolling quietly past our house, and on it our three logs. Beside the waggon a black fur cap swayed revoltingly to and fro.

"Yes. They're our logs," I replied icily. "What a – swine!"

"Swine! You swine!" cried little brother on the table and he drummed on the windowpane.

"You rotten swine!" my sister wailed, bursting into tears. "Your logs!" she hugged me as she cried.

"And Daddy's! Daddy's!" sobbed little brother who is now in Slovakia, and at this Mother hushed him because Dad was asleep in the next room after an attack of malaria.

"And Dad doesn't even know!" our sister wept in muted trepidation.

Mother shook her head helplessly, without a word; she looked so wounded that I couldn't bear it; I ran outside, climbed the back fence and raced ahead behind the barns. Then, arming myself with three sizeable stones, I waited till our logs came into sight through a chink in a barn door, whereupon I dispatched the stones on a curving course over the roof so rapidly that the last was in the air before the first had fallen. I didn't wait. I pelted away.

I know nothing. Nor had I any desire to know the result, that was not the point. My intention had been to provide an opportunity for Allah himself: I had placed three stones in his hand. It was, in any case, a wicked deed: why, I might have hit the horses!

And now, once more, the old meadow is within my field of vision, its biggest tree has long since been burnt in someone else's stove, but the farmer got what was coming to him, not that it was of any use to Dad, so what's the sense, anyhow? That I am, and we are here? And what have we got? In other words, what have we got from what we have? Why, even clean air is growing less plentiful! It's enough to make one howl with rage that no government has been set up that would be capable of guaranteeing quite simply the supply of air and water. Oh happy dreams, oh gilded lilies! Oh you lindens! What I see here, above all, is that no one allows the trees to mature, which makes my own prospects clear to me also. The great beeches behind Kanyur Hill are bowing to the mechanical saws, the slender grey pillars of those arches are crashing to the ground – if it were, at least, to some purpose, but like a needy family we devour almost all our substance without providing ourselves with anything durable, and that I never expected. And there was a hill that could have survived. Even Dad would have wondered at that.

Below the meadow, for instance, there is a copse, and today there is no well-spring there, but I know the spot precisely where just one prod with a pick would do the job. With the passage of time, however, wonderful undertakings have become pointless, so that were I today to take a pick, as I often feel like doing, I would be too late and instead of clearing the spring I would be indulging in sentimental folklore, and why? Because today meadows like that are no longer mown, they are left to decay, and if they are mown, people take along a crate of beer. Who is crazy? I am not ready to admit that I am, despite the fact that I shall be out-voted and, what is more, directed to the brewery. I know that when Gandhi revived hand-spinning, it served a militant purpose – to boycott something British. I'd willingly boycott things British! But I can't find anyone to join me, and there must be at least two for a boycott, and even then they would have to scowl a great deal if anyone was to notice their boycotting.

While pursuing these thoughts, which refuse to leave me even when I order them away, and which smear my better perceptions like tar on one's fingers, I was searching among the pepperwort for more rocks, I don't like poking about among the burdocks, and I piled some stones to hold back the water and from the bottom I scooped up sand mixed with black shells to cover them. Now, from behind the willows, an ordinary old man should appear, carrying a serviceable scythe over his shoulder, and as he walks past he should say:

"Building? Building?"

"Yes, I'm building, I'm building."

"Well, build away," he would say, having continued on his way without looking round, and I would be uncertain whether, for heaven's sake, it was true, or whether it had happened thirty years ago, which means now.

I glanced nervously towards the bank, and what did I see! Across the level tract bounded by a loop of the stream, where the ground is carpeted by pink-flowered shrubby restharrow among which an outspread coat was missing and on the coat Tonda was missing and many another player with pencilled cards made by cutting up school drawings, card players who should have been keeping the goats out of the clover, across this place came a group of people. My first impulse was, naturally, to get out of the water and to stop playing. Then I said to myself: Not a bit of it! – and the change can be ascribed solely to the fact that the whole world has gone crazy! Moreover, the group had already drawn nearer and among them I saw my friend Tonda.

"Hallo!" I called out faintly, in some embarrassment.

73

He nodded uncertainly and moved his lips, but the water drowned his words. For a while he gaped at me, then he raised his voice:

"That you?"

He scrambled down the steep bank to the stream. He looked around for a spot where he could deposit his uniform. Then, bare-foot and wearing nothing but shorts with braid at the sides, he ran to the pool and shouting, "Tatra photos, hold it!", he dived under water. The flash above the surface followed immediately. To myself I thought: time cannot be said to have diminished the significance of the performance, would that we had more policemen like this one.

Observing Tonda's nonchalant attitude towards his uniform and his office, I recalled his feelings when he first acquired them. And at once I was back in those bright, impetuous, hopeful days, and again I realized that I was growing old. Yes, I, too, am on the way out. Yet, there was no denying the happy thrill as I recalled how, after the liberation, we had been allotted a piece of meadowland. The effect it had on our family! How fervently we believed in the justice of history in the making, which would never recoil upon us, for this was our own history. I can recall again in all its plasticity, though it is no more than an image developed as if on a thermographic plate, my fearful delight at Dad's delight when he hurriedly planted twenty young fruit trees on our land. And I find myself regretting that I shall never own a meadow. I am surprised at myself, because I have always assumed hitherto that I am a part of what may be termed an aggregate man who owns an aggregate of meadows. Some central factotum having, however, kicked me out of that simple and pleasant equation, I have no say in the affairs of any meadow at all, which brings us, friends, to the birth of my shameful wish, which is this: somehow I really would like to have a meadow of my own. But to return: since we, too, had land at last, our status in the village rose.

Mother alone was unable to cope with the event. She required a natural explanation for it. This she found in the circumstance that the man appointed to the post of Minister of Agriculture must evidently be someone who had at some time seen her somewhere. Consequently, she feared that a change at the Ministry might install as Minister a fellow who had never seen her. And how right she was!

My visits home were infrequent. Each time I arrived, I learnt of surprising things. Geese were denied access to the village green, which was proclaimed a square. A factory was to be built. My schoolfellows had found themselves remarkable revolutionary jobs; Tonda timidly and proudly assumed his uniform, which really could signify that everything would be different, indeed, the exact opposite of what had been. In short, the entire community, having bestirred itself, had gradually come to rest some three degrees higher up. To find the family, I always had to go to the meadow. Mother would be turning the hay, or hoeing round the fruit trees, my brothers attacking the roots of invading bushes. Dad, of course, was always pottering around the oak trees with a view to using the lower shoots as winter fodder for the goats. Altogether, the meadow kept everyone occupied. But the plot next to ours had been allotted to a butcher who did nothing but clear the trees and sell the timber. Endowed with the bovine visage of a bully, he had anticipated the times correctly.

Once, I arrived home before Easter. I found more houses and more girls. I walked in a rather pleasantly expanded world and it looked as if this world would be wanting something nice from me. At home I learnt two weighty items of news: a linden by our window, which overshadowed us but official permission to fell it had not been forthcoming, had vanished from the row, and Dad was Chairman of the local Council. The first news, about the tree, cheered me not at all. The second did, a bit. And

Mother was darning by the window with a new alarm clock.

On another occasion I arrived for the summer holidays. The greening hillsides shaded away to blue, clouds skirted the horizon, the valley rang with the sounds of work, children shouted to each other in the lanes and all along the street it was the same, for instance, women were carrying baskets of bread dough to the bakery. I walked past the house which a young carpenter had built for himself. But his wife Vilma had died and he was left alone with their baby. His response to this misfortune was not of the happiest: he took to singing to himself. But the songs that he sang were not proper songs, they were his own shrunken thoughts: *First we saw it, then we plane it, then we go tack tack, and bring the shavings back* ... For that they tied him up and bundled him into a car. The carpenter has been in the lunatic asylum ever since and according to the doctors he is sane but for one small defect – he believes that his wife is still alive. I ask you, just for that! Instead of counting it to his credit! I arrived home, we had linoleum and the doors had been painted, my sister was bigger and nicer than usual, both brothers had their heads shaved in accordance with our summer tradition, again we owned no meadow, the linden trees along by the barns had almost finished flowering and on the field across the stream the referee was blowing his whistle.

Mother was washing-up, my sister drying for her.

I asked after Dad without the meadow.

"Hm! Well of course, he was sorry," Mother told me. "You could tell he was fretting, but all he said was: I'm a communist!"

"And tell him about that butcher next to us," my sister intervened.

"Well now, it was like this. I said to Dad: 'There you see that lout, at least he sold the timber and got some money.'"

"And what did Dad say to that?"

"Hm! He was cut up, you can imagine. All the sweat he'd put into it! First he said nothing, and then: 'Reckon he's the rascal, not me, he's the one to cry over it, not me.'"

My sister added:

"And all the time: 'I'm a communist, it's a duty.' So he's a communist!"

And Mother chimed in:

"He is that. How can I expect other folk to do things, he says, if I don't do them myself."

"And you, Mum?"

"Hm!" She waved a hand over the washing-up water. "Here today, gone tomorrow, that's how it is."

My sister laughed:

"Easy come, easy go, and there's bugger all to show."

Really it was all very simple and reasonable, on their side and on Dad's. I agreed with Dad.

"So that's an end to our gaffering," Mother concluded with a smile, and it was a co-operator's smile, because Dad had put her name down.

"He put your name down?" I asked in some surprise. "But you must've had to sign yourself surely!"

As she wiped the table, she tilted her head on her shoulder and considered:

"Well yes, of course I did. But ... hm, well he's a communist and ... and so are you, so what should I, you know?"

One of those days I took a turn at field work in Mother's place and I discovered that the co-operative farmers – teachers, the postmaster, a few clerks and workers' wives – were equipped just about at the horse-and-cart level. However, they were working with a will to acquire everything and to reap a better harvest than the private farmers, and to get it in earlier, too.

That first day at home, I asked Dad when he got back from the Council office:

77

"Why didn't you recruit a few farmers to start with?"

"My boy, we'd never have got started! The enemy is at work, you know, and we must keep forging ahead so long as things are moving. Like when you're pushing a heavy cart uphill – once you stop, you'll never shift it."

He was washing himself in the basin set on a chair, the muscles rippled beneath his skin as if he had come off a building site, instead of from the Council, and I was oppressed by a sense of inferiority: What if people's thoughts simply correspond to their muscle power and everything in philosophy, psychology etc. is merely a feeble compensation reaction, making a virtue of necessity, on the part of people aware that their muscles are not up to scratch?

"But take it psychologically, won't the farmers feel that a co-operative like that isn't their affair?" I asked.

He soaped his neck, the suds squelching under his hand, then with a brief upward glance, he said in a carefully restrained tone:

"Psychologically? They may get worried it'll work without them and against them, so they'll join."

"Maybe you're right, too," I said. And even from the back of his neck you could tell he was glad. By now I was so big and so grown-up that, alongside the disenchantment at seeing how limited was my father's freedom and independence, I was yielding to the painful realization that I would have, very quietly and inconspicuously, to be responsible for seeing that nothing happened to him. Yes, this I know today: the relationship between father and son can never be maintained at a level of genuine equality. The scales are simply tipped the other way.

He wiped the water from his eyes and said happily:

"After supper we'll talk it over. You've made an interesting point."

"We'll talk it over," I said.

"If only you'd waited with that co-operative ... " Mother chipped in to our conversation.

"Be quiet, nobody's asking you," he snapped, then he turned towards her and tried to speak more gently: "We're just discussing it together, my dear." He rinsed his hands. "You didn't think to ask Mum, then?" he said, and the face he pulled as he looked up at me was meant to suggest that that was a huge joke.

"But she's the member, not you," I remarked.

"There, you see," Mother said to me in a puzzled voice, "I'm the member, and I can't even open my mouth."

Dad rubbed himself dry and he gave out a healthy odour of body and soap and he laughed soundlessly. Then he said:

"Quite correct. You're the member, so go to the meetings and talk there. That's what we want, what we're fighting for, that our wives and mothers should get away from the kitchen and talk about the management of public affairs. Or haven't I ever said that?"

He buttoned up his clean shirt, turned to Mother and waited.

"Well, haven't I told you that twenty times at least?"

On receiving no answer, he left the room in a huff.

We carried the table out to the back, where in those days the setting sun still shone freely, and we had supper. Dad was cheerful again, Mother calm and the brothers were well behaved. There was a mildly festive air at supper, we were all together once more, in good health, I had just passed some exam or other, it was warm, order reigned in the cottage and there was piped water.

"Plenty of problems, my dear boy, but we're managing nicely," Dad said, happily surveying the scene; his eye lighted on the brother who is now in Slovakia, he grabbed him playfully by the scruff of the neck and shook him, "but it's growth we need, then pssst!" he whistled softly, and with an upward sweep of his strong right arm he lifted the roof a floor higher. "That's it, me lad!" he cried as he turned abruptly to his left and pinched my driver brother's nose, then my sister's. His radiant face evoked barely a smile from them. For a second he gazed sharply at them, then he pulled a face at my sister, who reciprocated and no more, so he shifted his chair to stretch his legs, and lighting a cigarette of the popular Partisan brand, he said with unconscious dejection:

"That's life!"

Mother sat, drumming her fingers on the table, limply and without rhythm. As I watched her, I felt she was avoiding my eyes. Suddenly she got up, glanced at me and started to clear the table. My sister helped her. All at once the brothers were gone from their places. Dad and I were alone and twilight was falling. Water murmured from across the fields, the lights went up at the mill. Bats were flying around. We sat there and it was all a long time ago, I was a little boy no more, but in the darkness beneath the lindens cycles wobbled on their way, their self-charging lamps wheezily buzzing, rabbits were thumping about in the shed, from a nearby barn someone was leading out cows unharnessed from a cart and a chain clanked as it shifted along the yoke, the acetone smell of paint wafted from the open doors of our house, and it suddenly struck me that the piped water, the new gate, the freshly painted doors, everything had been done in time for my holidays. All the signs at home indicated that things were really moving ahead in the right direction but, nevertheless, I was possessed by a vague, yet sweeping fear, in fact an actual anticipation of ruin looming over our home. I have often heard it said since that the nation sensed nothing, that people are simply being wise after the event, but I it was who lived in that cottage and sitting there with me at that moment was my father.

Dad let out a deep breath and coughed. In the darkness only his white shirt and his cigarette were visible. Mother passed behind us; as she returned, she said:

"Don't sit there, it's cold."

7

Sometimes one is surprised at oneself, at how one could have been so petty in relation to certain things and certain people, for my part I have often regretted things that have happened and ought not to have happened – that I have not always been able to live amicably – and now? Emptiness, mental anguish, yet time runs on like the tiny mechanism of a watch, clouds sail overhead, you pursue the flock of memories and in your heart it sounds like an amen. Something has gone, something frightful weighs upon the spirit, gone are the balmy evenings; turning to watch a passing cloud I send my greetings to those now far away, for, who knows, perhaps this selfsame wind will waft their way, this cloud perhaps may pass above their heads. As daylight fades and the cool of evening lies darkly in the valley, it is day for you, but my heart is heavy, because the eye cannot see so far; only in thought can I follow this wind and cloud. Thus the days drop into the sea of eternity and my time too will come, maybe, if that is to be my fate. As far as I am concerned, I am still in fair health, so the vultures and hyenas can lay no claim to me. But I would rather have the Caspian Sea behind me than before me, for as I see it, a man can travel over land on foot, whereas even our forefathers could not walk on the waters – that's how it was with him, with that other me, and I am beginning to be aware of it.

Not waiting for the final lectures of the year, I arrived home a few days before Christmas. Prague, that old wrinkled city with feet always chilled by the wind from the river and eyes filled with soot from the trashy coal which it tries to keep warm by, Prague disgusted me. Out in the country snow is lying on the fields, or at least an icy wind is whistling there, hoar frost crackles on last year's leaves, and here I walk the dirty streets past the closed shutters of pathetic little shops now ordered out of business, I go into the big shops only to retreat before the humiliating crush without buying a thing, I ride in the clanking tramcar where people are reading the bleak newspapers, scanning the columns for something to laugh at and not realizing that they are looking at it.

I arrived too early. The family had not had time to arrange the pre-Christmas order of things. Dad and I will go out into the space between the grey arc of sky and earth, where a black flock of ancient crows will be our sole companions. We shall climb the hill for a tree.

That we did not go and that for the first time in our lives we bought a Christmas tree must be blamed on our rapidly improving status in the community. Dad was now a district official. His shoes and his hat were the same as ever, that was not the point. This year, too, was the first in which Mother made no attempt to fatten a pig. She would have had to buy everything for it, and there was the snag; if one wants to show the farmers that the postmaster, the teacher and the worker's wife can also, by their joint effort, manage to till the soil, one can hardly expect the genuine farmers to sell grain and potatoes for one's pigs.

I had no idea that my family had experienced several exciting weeks that autumn. Reflecting today on the significance of past events, I realize that at the time I allowed the happenings in our village to be described quite inadequately to me, and my understanding of the information that came my way was primitive, probably comparable to the way the more foolish among us would still understand it today. It is not advisable to win. When they had sacked Dad from his post on the local Council, I was, in fact, glad to see him quickly promoted to office again. I regarded his triumph, erroneously, as a triumph. And he, too, succumbed to this error.

As I imagine it, his fall from the Chairman's seat went as follows:

"Chairman! Your delaying tactics are causing the rich farmers to laugh at us," they said, meaning that the farmers were cocking a snook at them.

The Chairman replied:

"In my opinion harsher measures against the farmers would evoke a psychological solidarity among them and against us."

"Hmmm! So is it this psychologicy stuff we're here for, or a class policy?" the committee boomed in Valachian dialect, and I will not go into detail, because if I did I would never get round to describing my visit to my brother the driver.

Less than a fortnight after Dad had fetched his tools from upstairs and set off as in the old days to a building job, they summoned him again and put him in charge of the building department at the District Council office. So a second confidence was reposed in him – yes, I know it would be more usual to say he enjoyed renewed confidence, but, after all, one speaks of a second reprimand. After a second expression of confidence, too, it is more difficult to slam the door.

On Christmas Eve we merrily sawed firewood. We fasted, but not a sign of the proverbial sucking pig for our pains, we decorated the tree, sang carols and hammered at nuts on the floor by the stove, with Mother eating Dad's kernels. On Christmas afternoon, all of us, except Mother, chased round the barns and snowballed like mad. "Dad, you're crazy," said Mother. My brothers could both hit the target with hard shots by now. "Fooling around, I get plenty of that with them," Dad said happily. And we enjoyed the Christmas festivities normally, as in the days when the world was under an obligation to us because it had a bad conscience on our account.

Not until St Stephen's Day did something from the new age occur. On St Stephen's Day, we had a visit from Uncle Balej who lived in the cottage by the brewery wall and who never, as the year was long, came to see us, although we had lived with him for a time after our parents' wedding, that is, our parents lived with him. Then the years passed. It was a spring evening with rain in the offing when Dad and I were on Uncle's field, tearing at the clover with both hands and stuffing it into a bag. How it happened we never understood, we had never been caught at anything before, but better to have been caught twice than to have it happen just then! For this undertaking was beneath us. We had always tended to correct the criminal negligence of landowners or we had sweated on other people's land since it was not vouchsafed to us to sweat on our own. On this occasion we had set out virtuously to gather dandelions, but with rain threatening it had been obvious that we could never get what we needed before the downpour. In short, we raised our heads and saw Uncle. "God be with you," was his greeting to us on his field. And never once did he refer to the matter. And as for us, the sense of shame never left us. When, yesterday, Cousin Karel invited me for a chat, and through the mask of ineffable sarcasm his smile of stony calm struggled to the surface by the wall, I was bound to recall this painful little incident, too, but that was nothing compared with what was to come; on St Stephen's Day, then, Uncle Balej paid us a visit.

"Brother-in-law," he turned to Dad, having placed his hat on the bed, seated himself and crossed his hands over his staff, "it's a pity we're brothers-in-law, otherwise I could speak more easily. What, I ask you, is the purpose in letting our cottage rot? To get me into the co-operative? Never! Not I nor any child of mine!"

As soon as I heard my uncle's words, I was deeply perturbed by them. And I had no inkling then that we were present at the birth of a stubborn resistance which would persist for decades, would seep from my uncle's head into the heads of all his family; that they would be barred from higher education, and get no permanent employment; that his sons and daughters would not marry, they would pay fines, buy themselves a television set, and all else they would lose or renounce, and proud Cousin Karel would end up as a labourer – that amazingly intelligent young man who, being a lad from a cottage where the only book was the prayer book, had once found an old Croatian almanac in somebody's attic and by repeated reading of this work had taught himself Croatian, but far and wide not a single Croat existed; it was the prelude to this saga that was now being written, as follows: the gable of Uncle's house had fallen, the chimney had collapsed, the damp interior reeked of smoke, the fire brigade had sued him, and the Council had refused him an allocation of a thousand bricks, a little cement and lime, because he had not signed an application to join the co-operative farm.

This was also the first time I had seen my father in action politically, and I certainly never guessed that there in our kitchen a little bud was swelling on a shockingly thrusting plant which was destined to invade half the arable land of Europe. Dad could have told uncle, truthfully, that he knew nothing about the rejection of his application, since it was a matter for the local Council. He could have said that he would make inquiries. That he would lodge a complaint at the District Office. Had he been somewhat longer in office, he would probably have advised his brother-in-law to put in a new application. But he could also have said that it was all nonsense, that he personally did not agree, but there was nothing he could do about it, or that there was some regulation or other. But no, he said none of these things.

"My dear Brother-in-law. If you were not my brother-in-law, you might not, perhaps, know what opinions I hold. But I am sure you know them, and therefore what I am about to say will not surprise you. Each one of us is a member of human society."

"Yes," my uncle nodded.

"And as such we receive and it is our duty to give. We are building a socialist order of society and you, dear Brother-in-law, should realize in good time, where you stand as a working man."

Uncle had been sitting erect in the chair, his hands on his staff, his hat beside him on the bed. Now he rose with a calm air and walked towards the door, where he turned to say:

"Well, that's what I needed to know. From you, Brother-in-law, I want nothing, why, I know you, you have nothing, any more than we have. I simply wanted to find out what it's about in my case, the building material or politics." He picked up his hat. "Well, I'll wish you good-bye. Happy New Year."

He left.

I was sitting on the bed, Dad at the table, Mother on the wood-box, my sister was out with her girl friends, the brothers were tobogganing. The old alarm clock rattled and shook, it pointed to three in the afternoon, and the new one more quietly to ten minutes earlier, the kitchen range was still hot from cooking dinner, a plate with slices of Christmas bread stood on the table, a copy of *The World of the Soviets* lay on the windowsill, and under the coat-rack lay the cat. The new water taps glistened. Mother said:

"Oh Dad! Now I see, you're not kind."

"Mum!" I said.

Because this would never have happened if I had not chanced to be there. Probably Dad had felt obliged in my presence to adopt some kind of principled attitude. Had Uncle Balej arrived on another Sunday afternoon when I would have been in Prague, at the cinema, because at that time of day my colleague Rudolph was always quietly making love to his girl in our room so that she could be home early, then Dad might have said, "Brother-in-law,

it's not my fault, I'll make inquiries, I can't promise anything," and Elishka would be walking downstairs two
steps ahead of Rudolph, bells ringing in her heart.

"No!" Dad shouted. "I'm not kind. To your mind I'll
never be kind!"

He threw the words half-way between himself and
Mother. His glance at me was agitated. There is a terrible
strength in me, and I think I know why. I don't want it,
but it is there, and this ageing man will want, come what
may, to go under with dignity.

"I'm not acting on my own behalf, you know!" Again
he sought my agreement with his eyes. "The comrades
appointed me."

"Well, whoever did the appointing," Mother said
peaceably, "all I know is you're always mean to my family.
Now, if it'd been one of the Tarandova lot . . ."

That was a cruel untruth. In time, in a year or two, they
came pleading from Tarandova, and he acted no
differently.

He sent the stool flying as he jumped up.

"Stuff and nonsense! There we have your chicken
brains! Society and the working class come first with me!
And in second and other places brother-in-law and the
entire family!"

I kept quiet.

"Aren't I right?" In full flight, he turned to me and
halted.

"No," I said, mainly because that was the most important, although it certainly was not everything. But it was
the harder end of the stick.

He stood there staring at me. Then moving towards the
door, he took his overcoat and his hat.

"Good night all," he said, in the afternoon.

I watched Mother drooping minute by minute in mind
and body. More and more lifeless as time went by, she
clung to the wood-box. And Christmas was no more than
voices outside our windows. We drew the blinds and

switched on the electric light. I was getting hungry, too, but it seemed out of place to mention such a paltry need just then. Mother aimlessly stoked the fire.

"When will he be back?" I asked.

"Hm," she waved a feeble hand, "tomorrow morning, maybe."

That I had not realized. I really had not realized anything of the kind.

The brothers arrived, their boots soaked, they dried themselves all over, and they were hungry. My sister came, immediately putting her cold hands on my cheeks and under my shirt and showing her affection by calling me rude names. Then she took off her coat and as she was hanging it on the rack, she asked:

"Where's Dad?"

"Out," Mother replied.

"Lads, take my advice," my sister said to the brothers, "say your prayers, pee and to bed, look sharp!"

Prayers said, peeing done, they had not yet left the room when Dad appeared. And as if nothing had occurred.

"Good evening! Ah, my lassie is home! And my son, too, and my wife, good evening *chanum*. 'Pon my word, I'm glad to be home, the world outside is vile."

Still in his coat, he sat down at the table.

The lads were about to slip away, but he saw them and rebuked them:

"What, no goodnight to Dad?"

They went to him. He caressed them. The boys left the room. Dad stood by the table, leaning on it with both hands and rocking backwards and forwards from toes to heels. His teeth began chattering, grating as he shivered. He shut his eyes, he was pale and tired.

"You've got malaria?" Mother remarked.

He turned silently towards her.

I wished she hadn't said that, because he was trying to make it up.

"See that?" He turned confidentially to me. "I've no

home, I tell you. Even a horse has a home, a cricket has a home . . ."

"Don't stand there blathering, clear off to bed," said Mother, and the veins in her neck were pulsing.

Not even looking at her, he addressed me.

"Hear that? Clear off!" he imitated, pursing his lips. "Clear off yourselves, *hombre*!" and he dragged a revolver from his pocket.

Icily and as though by no will of my own I held out my hand. He reversed the gun and handed it to me.

"Want to have a shot? You're my son. My firstborn."

Maybe I failed to understand, maybe it is only now that I understand correctly, at that moment I said:

"Here? Outside."

We went outside, I trailing the revolver clumsily through the air against my thigh, catching a fleeting glimpse of Mother's horrified expression; out at the back it was dark, only the mill showed a light, the stream was not babbling, it was frozen. Dad stepped aside to the fence and began to piddle, I followed suit, the revolver in one hand, and thus occupied I remarked:

"You can't go about it like that. Even if you were in the right."

"I didn't have to, mate. But I'm not sorry. That brother-in-law, I respect him as a craftsman and a tough fellow. But during the war, when we had nothing to eat, they had enough. When your mother and I were building this cottage, we had to run up debts on all sides, with him too. And no sooner was I away in Iran, than they came dunning. No regrets. Not to mention that it's class justice."

"Do you remember that clover?" I said. I thought he might comfortably forget about the revolver.

"Give it here," he said.

I handed it over obediently. Our eyes had adjusted, it was no longer so dark, where snow lay it was twilight. I should have returned to the kitchen, to say a word in the midst of this horror. But I was afraid to leave him. He released the safety catch, fired, and again, and I said nervously:

"The brave placed an arrow in his bow, when suddenly a shot rang out!"

If she had not dropped dead in there, she might hear us, I must speak as loudly as possible.

"My turn, Dad, give it to me."

I fired twice.

"You have a revolver?" I asked.

"For the job. We're at risk. They attacked one of the comrades after a meeting in Tarandova."

"What did they do to him?"

"Nothing. Beat him up. Well, what of it!"

I had an idea.

"What about going for a walk?"

"We could do that," he said gladly.

"But we'll have something to eat first, won't we?"

"We can eat."

I clutched at the hope that in this way things would slip back to normal and everything would be wiped out, or at least assume the accustomed image.

My sister was sitting at the table, head in hands like an old woman, Mother must have been in the next room.

"Give us a bite to eat, lass," Dad said, in the non-political vernacular now. She rose without a word.

I went into the next room, expecting to find Mother weeping terribly, but I was wrong. In the dark, she was getting the bed ready for the night, she didn't want to turn round, but she did, to see who was there. As I drew closer, I could see her in the dim light from the kitchen; she was gazing at me, her movement arrested, her eyes darkly shining, her shoulders soft, her hands, holding a bundle of linen, sagged, she appeared about to take a step towards me, but that I did not want to happen; as I came quickly to her, she laid her head on my shoulder, her arms hanging loosely, I embraced her head, which I had never done since childhood, and now, at last, she wept terribly. And I with her.

"Dad and I are going for a walk," I said afterwards.

He was there, waiting for me outside, supper again untouched on the table. He was leaning against the corner of the house and smoking.

"All that will be cleared away one day," he gestured vaguely in the direction of the barns, which, due to causes defying detection, were burnt out a year later.

We stepped out on the road. We were completely sober. Under the arching lindens, whose bare branches met overhead, the darkness was somewhat deeper.

"When work starts on the drainage, the lindens will go west," he pointed his cigarette at the trees, which within two years had gone west.

Walking slowly, we reached the weir where the Pukysh family lived. In the pearly light filtering through the clouds, the basket-maker's home could really have been in the Klondyke. The shack was in darkness, only the whitish smoke was busily puffing from its tin chimney. Ice broke beneath the weir and we could hear the muted flow of water. We stopped by the backwater.

"We'll have to regulate the stream again," Dad said, and as he spoke, the fish vanished; "and straighten that path," and the line of apple trees toppled to the ground; "and one day, maybe, we'll lay a branch line on the other side to the factory," he said, and a hideous embankment of slag bulged over the mill-race.

"Many tasks await us," he frowned, "and we have many enemies," he said, and Mother died.

And so we stepped out into the future and simultaneously towards Tarandova. We walked slowly, he continually adjusting his step to mine, which I have always taken to mean that I should keep in step with him. And so we came to the next weir, where I am now standing in the water absorbed in play and in memories of many other happier things than those of which I am now writing. Here

91

the spreading valley resembled a bowl, with strips of wood-land weaving down its easy slopes to plunge into the channels of the streams, while the bushes bordering the fields, known in these parts as holts, traced graduated transections. It was to this slanting hill country, now white in the light of the newly risen moon, that Dad pointed.

"Some day we'll put powerful, very powerful tractors, you know, to work here, to plough it right across."

I believe I said nothing to this, it seemed right to me and it was foolish of me to feel sad.

Suddenly he left the path to cross a snowy field in the direction of the stream, a bit above the weir, a place where the ground sags gently. Pointing to that place he led my eyes along the loop made, evidently, by the stream at some time, which I had never noticed before. At the highest point of the loop, now furrowed by the plough, below the steep bank where the path runs, stood, unaccountably and strangely isolated, a misshapen willow, bent by a pile of stones gathered from the field.

"There, where you see the deep water," he motioned towards the ground below the willow, where water there was none, "I used to catch fish there. And what fish!"

"Like what?"

"Like this," beaming happily, he showed a width three feet with his hands.

I looked towards the willow.

"It's not true any more," he said casually. We returned slowly to the weir, and suddenly he seemed to me to be weaker and better, not dangerous at all, maybe we had simply been for this walk and nothing else had happened that evening. Suddenly he halted and looked at me in surprise.

"Fifteen years! Fifteen years ago I was in Iran."

I could think of nothing to say to that. He was – fifteen years ago. Today, however, I know why the thought struck him and what lay behind his words, for today I under-stand infinitely more about the patterns that our life is assuming. I have realized that sometimes one is surprised at oneself; at how one could have been so petty in relation to certain things and certain people, for my part I have often regretted things that have happened, and ought not to have happened – I have not always been able to live amicably – and now? Emptiness, mental anguish, yet time runs on like the tiny mechanism of a watch, clouds sail over head, something has gone, something frightful weighs upon the spirit, gone are the balmy evenings. Thus the days drop into the sea of eternity and my time will come, too, maybe, if that is to be my fate. As far as I am concerned, I am still in fair health, so that the vultures and hyenas can lay no claim to me . . . With the exception of that Caspian Sea, which does not lie before me, as it lay before him, and of the hyenas whose insatiable claims could not touch the living.

He stepped out again, and I with him.

"So, my boy, time was when I was in Iran . . . I had malaria, it's just not true any more!" he said bitterly. And as if he were quite alone, he sighed: "Life is so very, very foul!"

Fear assailed me once more – a double-layered fear, of him and for him. And I could no longer contain my grief at the thought that my help is of no avail and all my people must submerge themselves utterly and completely in their precious misfortune. I shouted:

"Tatra photos, hold it!"

I thrust my head under water to accomplish the shameless somersault in the manner of happy Tonda in the days before the uniform.

When I raised my head again, it was to meet the horrified gaze of the entire hall.

8

My first impulse was to get out of here!

Nevertheless, I returned past the long rows of tables to my place and it seemed to me that I had been away somewhere for a long, long time and that meanwhile everything had changed. Every step lent force to the looming sense of guilt and with it my friends receded from me. Never before had I felt myself utterly abandoned, although I was aware that such a state can exist. Just as other things we merely know about exist – artificial limbs, for instance. Everyone knows that artificial limbs exist, but none of us want to relate their existence to ourselves in particular. I would venture to bet, however, that any one of you, on being fitted with a limb, will say in the corridor of the clinic: As if I hadn't known this from the outset! Yes, yes, and yet we always tend to behave as if the worst could never happen, while under our indulgent eyes our future misfortune is swelling in the bud.

Ah well! I returned and there was a strange calm at our mineral-water-bespattered table; when any of my colleagues happened to meet my eyes, they smiled faintly like men who really could not find it in them to be angry with me. People in the hall had relapsed into apathy, apart from a few tables where they showed some animation about affairs of their own. Another speaker took the platform and I doubt if the drivel he let loose could be matched in all the world. I was alone in listening to him; my hope was that by diligently cutting myself down to fit his subject matter I could become inconspicuous.

However, I had not known that the next speaker was to

be our chief. As he rose and walked to the platform, I felt that my colleagues were saying, without looking at me: So you see! But they were mistaken. The chief laid his notes on the stand and announced that he did not intend to refer, there and then, to my speech, because he did not wish to improvise in replying to serious words which were evidently the result of lengthy consideration. I was incapable of deciding immediately how to take this statement, especially the part about my words being evidently the result of lengthy consideration. A cold breath chilled me, that was all. When I mentioned loneliness just now, I was merely voicing the fear of it. Now it was actually here. Now I would be completely alone; not even my sense of guilt, nor any desire for forgiveness that might possess me, could alter that, because feelings like that could help no one. I had put everyone in danger, that I must realize and I must allow nothing to surprise me and nothing should seem to me unjust. All I had to do from now on was keep cool and stand my ground, showing no concern for my own welfare; ultimately we all have to realize that life is no joy-ride, and now it is my turn, at last I am in danger – at last. And I must show consideration for them, lest they think I am conceited. Grant me the gift of humility, O Lord, I would say if I had one to say it to.

After these disgustingly messianic words of truth, I see that I shall have to speak other words of truth, in explanation. One winter morning, I set out on one of my frequent journeys. The exhilaration I always experience when motoring cancelled my habitual stage-fright about the job ahead. I was going to see a girl who, as usual, would not be as I imagined from her letter; this girl had been turned down at her interview for admission to high school. The route led through gently rolling country with red patches of newly built co-operative cow-sheds at the approaches to the villages, until we reached the small town, which possessed one of every type of shop. That is how it always is. And we always start by having lunch in the restaurant, then I go about my business while my driver sits in the car, observing the passers-by until he falls asleep.

Immediately I saw the uncomely girl I decided that she could not have deserved to fail the examination. It also occurred to me at once that the quality of derision which had breathed from her letter was not discernible in her face. And altogether, she appeared to be much less affected by the matter about which she had complained.

"We received your letter, Comrade," I said, and the light reflecting from the snow in the back yard fell into the room.

"Please sit down," she said. "That letter?" she laughed indulgently, as though I was the one to have made a fuss, not she. "I wrote simply to show you that in any case you won't do anything."

"I won't? Or who?" I replied, and I noticed how their dog was observing me.

"I don't know . . . someone, whoever writes the final decisions," she looked at my overcoat, "I don't know how to say it, someone higher up – I don't know whose job it is," she said.

She was a rare type, a girl born for a hard life, if not for something worse.

"You're right," I answered. "But it's not true that we won't do anything. What is true is that whatever we can do has no effect. Tell that to everyone you talk to, will you? Where's your dad?"

"It's all different somehow," the girl said uncertainly. "My worries are different to what you think they are, and I had no idea about yours. Dad is at work."

Leaving the girl, I directed my steps to the school which, it seemed, she was not to attend. One of the unobjectionable young misses showed me where their headmaster was to be found. I entered into his presence. Many headmasters today look like anyone but a headmaster. I know this, but it always hits me in the eye, just the same. It is almost unthinkable that they might collect minerals or start up a choir in the town. From the face of this headmaster, too, I could see that he had lost the ability to cuff a pupil without having gained the ability to inspire through a consuming passion for his subject. Though paralysed from the outset by futility, I started negotiations. The headmaster blankly refused, however, to show me the examination results, he merely babbled something about the all-round assessment of candidates. With hatred in my heart, I put a test question:

"What, Comrade, do you find unattractive about the Minister of Education?"

He looked into his drawer, at the papers on his desk, but he found nothing in that line and that was enough for me – no, he was not capable of making an all-round assessment. Bidding him an icy farewell, I emerged into the fresh air.

When I reached the car, I woke the driver, he turned the heating on for the windscreen and we drove along the slushy street. How well I know these homeward journeys! The feeling that there had been no need to travel anywhere, that I had known it all before, but I had had to go in order to be able to say with full responsibility that there had been no need to go. And now came the dreary job of writing something which could be printed, but would nevertheless allow me to preserve some modicum of integrity. At least I was going home, to my children who are always puzzled about the kind of work I do, what my position actually is and what the fruits of my labour. While attempting by the fullest definitions to give them their bearings in their country, I worry that my precise descriptions may cause them to wonder whether things may, after all, not be quite as I have said. So we journeyed, with one duty remaining – to stop in the regional capital where at the reception desk of the Regional Council I would sign the register which gave official approval to my visit. I could have done this on the outward journey, but I usually wait until I know the result of the day's work; if I have had a conflict on the job, I sign up, but if not, we carry on and no one knows we have been around.

Dusk was falling and car lights advanced upon us from the swirling wet snow, I scrambled out of the water, the mud I had stirred up settled, slowly I dressed and as I was leaving the weir a shoal of tiny fish returned from the shelter of the bank to the surface. I'm glad I'm not in Prague, I whispered, and as I looked around it seemed almost impossible that Prague could really exist.

The day the article about the girl appeared, the School Inspector exclaimed:

"A tramp like that has no place in any school!"

"You mean the headmaster?" But nobody asked the Inspector that – everyone knew who he meant.

The grave insult came to the ears of the girl's father, and he packed his daughter off to the doctor. After which he intended to sue. The doctor's finding that the daughter was *intacta* moved the Chairman of the District Council, too, to anger. He announced that it was not valid and had the girl called before a medical panel. She refused to attend, whereupon, next day, a policeman entered her home to explain to her that the honour of many people was at stake. At this she obeyed the order, and having been left in the waiting-room whence all the far happier patients had long since departed, this girl, who in childhood had lost her mother, jumped out of the window and was killed. I think that her father, on returning home from the afternoon shift to find his daughter missing, must have gone to look for her. But he learnt nothing. All night he worried and in the morning he went to the police, who told him nothing because they were at a loss how to do it. Only after anxious discussion in other quarters did they call him and I think they said to him:

"Please take a seat."

He took a seat. With one hand he proffered his identity card across the desk to the officer, with the other, in which he was holding his cap, he wiped the sudden sweat from his brow. They knew him, so they were merely checking that he was carrying his own identity card, not someone else's. And in fact they probably just did not know how to proceed. At last the officer said:

"Your daughter has met with an accident."

And all present unhappily moistened their lips. Then Tonda said:

"Let's be frank – you must admit that you failed in your parental duty by letting your daughter jump out of a second-floor window."

"I?" asked the father, and asked no more.

I walked along the sunflower field towards the wood, all the golden heads were turned one way and above them a drowsy buzzing. This is where we used to race after our goats to get them quickly into the woods and out of sight. For no farmer liked to see us near his fields. Goat-boys – bad boys. I turned to Tonda, who was chucking clods at his bearded devils to drive them into the shelter of the trees, and when they were there, Tonda, having a clod left, aimed it at my old nanny. She was walking with her usual slow sagacity, her knees cracking, she was chewing, not anticipating anything of the kind, and when the clod thudded on her belly she fled in terror, desperately straining her hind legs to get up the bank. It made me furious, and I was sorry for Mother who prized our old nanny so highly, so I yelled at Tonda for being such a bloody fool. He laughed and aimed a loose clod at me, it disintegrated into grass roots as it flew, earth got into my hair and Tonda squealed with laughter as he ran into the wood to collect heavy fir cones as ammunition against me. I collected stones.

"Bloody fool," I roared, and he laughed and threw fir cones from under the trees. With the first stone I scored a direct hit, so hard that bark flew from the trunk of the tree, and I was relieved that I hadn't missed, because otherwise Tonda would have got it. He started to swear terribly. I hit again with awful precision, till the wood showed white beneath the bark, but fear, growing minute by minute, was clutching at my throat.

"How dare you throw things at my goats!" I yelled stupidly, because usually we pelted our goats whenever necessary.

Tonda bent down for a stone and aimed it straight at my legs. He laughed, but by now fear and rage sounded in his laughter. I knew that this time I would aim right at him, therefore with a last flash of sense I dropped my stone and grabbed a stick. It spun twice in the air. I thought it had barely touched Tonda, but he huddled on the ground, head in hands and boo-hooed. I stood in trepidation some ten yards from him, reminding myself that he shouldn't bash our goats. Then I crept nearer, and my hope that Tonda was simply putting it on left me.

"What's wrong?" I asked crossly.

He spoke indistinctly, he boo-hooed and felt his back. I saw several jagged tears in his shirt. He certainly was not yet aware how torn it was. When his groping had given him some idea of the damage, he cried even more and he jerked out:

"Ow, what d'you know, the way our Mum and Dad sweat their guts out!"

At these words I sat down – I would never have expected them.

"I mayn't tear my shirt," Tonda boo-hooed, helplessly reaching over his shoulder to his back, where blood was welling up from the scratch.

Then I started crying, and the two of us sat there boo-hooing in the wood, but my reasons were so unacceptable that Tonda, with bubbles at his nose, was soon giggling:

"Why're you crying, silly, it isn't your fault!"

I started to laugh, too, then we discovered that the goats had gone, they were out in the open again. We drove them under the shelter of the trees and went to watch newts in the well. They were there, they walked and swam, and they gave absolutely no indication that twenty-five years later someone would be saying to me:

"Did you sign the register?"

"I did," I replied with grim foreboding.

"But on the way home," said the chief. "Come to my room, all of you. That girl must have done something."

He was upset, almost pale with excitement. His eyes strayed involuntarily to the neon clock over the door, as though the ghostly march of its figures as they lit up and faded away marked the passage of an unstated time limit during which we had to perform an appropriate task, and we knew not what.

"What did she do?" I asked.

"We have been strictly forbidden to take any interest in her. So don't ask me, I know nothing, even the Director doesn't know. You've seen her, you've spoken to her. What did she seem like?"

"She wasn't very good-looking, she was intelligent, she had only a father. She seemed born for a hard life, if not for something worse."

"All right, then, the girl's done something. But why do we get the blame again?" Slavek wondered.

"Poor fellow, it's your first day here, isn't it?" the chief sneered. "Look sharp and ditch any critical stuff you may be working on and rustle up a concern with some success to its name, that's what we're all going to need, desperately."

"Idiot, you should have signed up on the way there," Slavek said to me. "Then it stands to reason nothing could have happened."

"I'm delighted that you're so helpful," the chief said with disappointment and he added: "Please don't underestimate the signing up. I know as well as you do that it's nonsensical, but since the thing exists, keep to it. After all, we want to make the paper as good as we can. Or don't we?"

No one spoke. We want to.

"Do you know, Chief, I'm not really sure if I want to any more," Slavek said after a pause.

"We need to find out what happened," I said. "I'll go there."

"That'll be the best!" the chief's voice rose to a shout, and he got up from his desk. "As it is we'll spend six months squaring things on your account!"

"For God's sake, don't do any squaring!" I, too, shouted. "I'm not asking you to!"

"Oh well," the chief remarked casually, "who says it's on your account? You've nothing to fear, your father was working class and that'll cut some ice for a while yet."

The road to the little town where I hoped to find out what the girl had done was frozen and sprinkled with cinders. Not wanting to wait for the connection, I walked the last stretch through country which pleased me not at all, and everything I passed looked exactly as though it belonged to nobody. Fences, houses, village inns, fruit trees, sheds for drying fire-hoses, bridges over the ditches, neglected fountains, wooden shelters at bus stops, bursting bags of fertilizer, fractured cement pipes, barns, schools, churches, committee rooms, smithies, railings by a stream, the croaking of public-address systems, war memorials, derelict threshing machines, purple-complexioned personages on motor-cycles, blocks of masonry, beams of wood, fish ponds, works of peasant architecture, surgery hours, repair shops, tool depots, retaining walls at road bends, incinerators of letters, opinions of the young, an old organist, steel constructions to support festive decorations at the approaches to a village on public holidays, wooden barrels, weeping willows, rings for tethering horses at the corners of hostelries, rusty and twisted cables on flagpoles, tar barrels, *anno domini* in the asbestos roofs, heaps of compost, pigeon-holes of outdated complaints, tyres, garbage tips of personal ideals, the Czech countryside. All this was exactly as though it belonged to nobody, it conveyed

nothing to me, or perhaps I have already become cor-
rupted and deaf. When, now and then, a lorry passed me,
the diesel smoke hung over the road, not budging, however hard I kicked it. Whose it is, whose is it! I screamed.
Let him stop it. Who does he think he is, anyhow! But,
apart from the wires stretching over fields furrowed by the
broad, deep tracks of tractors cruising at will, there was
nothing. Neither crows nor rooks were here, those endearing birds, and I should not wonder a bit if the girl were
dead.

I arrived in the town and, indeed, it was so. I had
planned to make various careful inquiries. Now I ditched
all that and anger drove me straight to the police.

"What's supposed to be going on here?" I asked.

"Hullooo, there!" someone thrust his right hand at me,
and it was Tonda, the old pal.

"I don't give a damn about that," I replied. "I refuse to
go on just registering things!"

"I heard something, is it true, that your Dad may have
died?" Tonda said.

"Long ago. Five years ago," I replied and soon I
departed.

I considered it my duty to speak with the doctor who
had examined the girl in the interests of her reputation,
only they had promptly transferred him elsewhere, and
nobody wanted to tell me where. I went back to my old
pal, he immediately got the address for me, I travelled to
the place, but what was the use, since the doctor was afraid
to talk to me. He calmed down only when I had spoken as
follows:

"I come to you as one who has no official interest in the
matter, in fact I have been expressly forbidden to ask
about it."

"Please sit down," she said. "That letter?" she laughed
indulgently, as though I was the one to have made a
hysterical fuss, not she. "I wrote simply to show you that
in any case you won't do anything."

"I won't? Or who?" I replied and as I spoke the dog was observing me.

"I don't know," she replied in confusion, "someone – I don't know whose job it is."

"Whose is it, whose is it! Let him stop! Who does he think he is, anyhow!" I screamed and I kicked at the diesel smoke, but it wouldn't budge from the road.

"I understand it now," the doctor said.

"I don't, I don't!" I replied.

He hunched his shoulders in alarm, then he brought out with difficulty:

"So now . . . I shall tell you how it was. She was not a virgin, though for her father I certified that she was."

At first I failed to grasp the significance of what he was saying. Then I jumped up and pointed at him:

"I see! So when they called her before the panel, all she could do was to jump out of the window. Admit it!"

"You are an informer, traitor and collaborator," he hissed at me. "You wrote about her intentionally. Admit it!"

I sank back into the chair. He was terribly right, I had written about her intentionally.

"Doctor," I said, mustering a feeble retort, "are you so stupid that you can't recognize a virgin when you see one?"

"Of course I can!" He darted from his seat and started pacing the store room in which he lodged. "Ssss!" he hissed, then he collapsed on the bed. "What could I do? Why even so she was far more of a virgin than those scoundrels, the elected representatives of the people!"

"I know," I said after a brief silence. "You just had to give her a certificate."

"That's right!" he cried with great hope and he offered me a cigarette.

When I had left him, I saw that it was dark and I had nowhere to spend the night. I went upstairs again.

"Have you by any chance," I said, "have you any photos of floods, please?"

"Certainly, I have," he said with surprise, "I have a lot of photos of floods, do you want to see them? And then you could stay here for the night."

He took pleasure in showing me colour slides which he had taken of many and various floods throughout his life. He was an old doctor and he had seen a number of floods. I stayed the night with him.

Next day I made use of the other address given me by an old pal, although he was not allowed to do so. I went to the regional town. The psychiatrist whom I sought out was a naïve old chap: he imagined that the newspapers wanted to write about the place of gardening in the treatment of less serious mental illnesses. He conducted me round the hospital park, showed me how their roses were protected and the young fruit trees wrapped up, I saw the trimmed shrubberies, I noted how the trees were pruned, nor did I fail to observe the treatment of compost, I visited the glasshouses where the fine dew sprinkling the lettuces misted our spectacles as well, but we laughed at that. Then he took me to the workshops where several patients were repairing tools in preparation for spring which was waiting at the gates of that madhouse.

"There is the man you asked about. He's almost recovered now," he said. "The only question is whether the collapse may not recur when he learns that his daughter is dead."

"You think he doesn't know?"

"I know he doesn't know."

"Then why does he think he's here?"

"He is under the impression that he committed an aggressive act from political motives."

"From political motives?"

"That was in him. But it is merely the present-day manifestation of something that goes much deeper."

"What do you mean by that?" I asked this psychiatrist.

"I have no liking for the present fashion of explaining everything in terms of current social problems. You, too, it seems to me, are tending that way."

"And do you want to exclude the social factors?" I asked this psychiatrist.

"Look at it this way. Who can say that natural selection is finished. Time was when its instrument was the climate, for instance. The instrument today is – if you like – the factor of social pressure. The source must be sought in organization, nutrition, the state of health, in the changing mode of production, but they all add up to that destructive social violence."

"You hit on that by yourself?"

"Nobody discovers anything alone! The idea is current in the world, in fact it comes from the West. I am appalled by the West; it is suffering from a total paralysis of the linkage between recognizing one's condition and action to regulate it. I prefer – do you know what?" He stopped in the middle of the garden path and turned to me with a quizzical air. "I prefer that we should remain in a state of pleasant backwardness. What do you say to that! Russia will survive the collapse of the so-called industrial society chiefly because she hasn't experienced its full impact, consequently she will be materially and spiritually fit to adopt the system that is bound to be born of the collapse."

"And what about us in the meantime?"

"As I have said – those who don't let themselves be destroyed will survive. In other words, those who can come to terms with the facts without trauma."

"Tell me, do you regard the things people are doing outside the gates of your institution as a coming to terms with the facts, or as giving shape to these awful facts?"

"Sir, I believe in viewing matters squarely and I am a dialectician, so I say – they are doing both! Whoever is afflicted by the facts is ready to acknowledge their existence, which is the best thing he can do. But he who is creating these facts is not yet ready to take cognizance of them. By his deeds he reaches outwards, he feels no inner pain and there is no point in bringing it home to him and saying: 'All in good time!' You, however, belong to a third type, you are creating facts for yourself and for others while, simultaneously, you are gravely afflicted by them and you are incapable of adapting to them. I expect to see you here in time."

"And you, for your part, Doctor, are a happy man in view of what is coming," I told this psychiatrist.

"What is coming, may I ask?"

"An amendment to the law on the management of institutional parks and gardens. Every institution will be placed under a Steering Committee set up by the local agricultural co-operative. So that, on the agricultural side, therapy will be in the hands of the co-operative farm."

"It's not possible, they can't do that . . ." He gaped at me in horror and then he added with resignation in his voice: "They can, I know they can . . ."

And as I was leaving that therapeutic garden, I suddenly recalled an event which had faded from my memory long ago and nothing had ever happened to remind me of it. In our street there lived a young carpenter whose wife died after the birth of their child. The carpenter lost his mind and took to singing. The horrified citizens, to whom it would never have occurred to sing in the circumstances, saw to it that he was put in an asylum. By now he has been there thirty years, if he has not died. Apparently he soon regained his health, except for the belief that his wife was still alive. But, above all, there were grave fears about what he might do should he, on coming home, meet any of the men who had bound him and loaded him into that car. A very real fear, I should say! And it cannot be otherwise!

Leaving that therapeutic garden, I was haunted by the thought that I might, in similar manner, find myself under treatment at any time, at any time at all! Whenever I

allow it to happen. At any moment, if any one of us con-
ducts himself in accordance with his inner being, they can
send him for treatment, and thirty years later they will
still be unable to let any of us go home for fear that we
may meet them – we'd be so bloody angry! '

Twelve people, and all their voices raised against me. I
could feel how, under the impact of the barrage, quietly
and one by one, any hands that might have wished to lend
me incorporeal support were withdrawing from me. The
old packer lady from Dispatch was in tears – she was fond
of me, she said, but where was I heading if I could speak as
I had at the conference about things that should be sacred
to all of us! One of the older functionaries, for his part,
was anxious to address a few friendly words to me, perhaps
it was not too late. Then for ten minutes he delivered an
impassioned speech, drawing a parallel between my so
disgraceful pronouncements and his own life. Finally, he
put the rhetorical question whether anyone present wished
to tell him that he had not conducted himself in a correct
and upright manner.

"My friends," said the Director of the Newspaper
Trust, when at last his turn came to speak. "I cannot find
words to express adequately my appreciation of the sincere and critical spirit inspiring this conference of ours. In
the first place, I wish to stress that I shall certainly defend
our colleague against anyone who might wish to attribute
to him hostile intentions. There can be no doubt about his
sincerity."

Whenever anyone takes to defending me and bases his
entire defence on a belief in the sincerity of my intentions,
things have always turned out badly. For it always tran-
spires that apart from the pious intention, there is
absolutely nothing good in me and, above all, that there is
nothing about which I am right. Consequently, I knew
immediately that I could take little pleasure in the
Director's speech for the defence – in fact, almost none.

"On the other hand, however, we cannot persist for ever

in taking a sincere intention as an excuse for every mistake," the Director continued excellently and as I had expected, "for it is the result that counts, and whoever is the author of the intention must honestly admit his authorship of the result as well . . ."

I looked into the faces of my colleagues because I had resolved to do so. They were, I think, sad and dignified. That, too, was the only way for me to bear myself, then and for ever after. Suddenly I felt at ease, peace flowed through my vitals, my eyes strayed casually, seeing the waiters who, oblivious to what was afoot, were moving from table to table collecting the coffee cups, while my ears received the entire sound of the hall, so that alongside the Director's voice from the loudspeakers I heard its original at the microphone and on the stairway outside the swing doors a cleaner was filling a bucket with water.

And therefore everyone can believe me when I say that I awaited, with no sense of anxiety, the words which had to follow, and that in view of their exceptional nature I actually looked forward to their chilling impact on all the people and colleagues who were glad that these words were not being spoken about themselves. Nor about me, colleagues and gentlemen, nor about me! I am no longer the man who entered this hall, I am now reaping what I've sown for myself. I am a man who has set a trap behind him to make himself afraid to turn back. I am weak, yes, and I am afraid, yes, but the fear is all around me; no quarter offers me the promise of a better way out and that is, after all, true freedom, to face equal danger wherever one goes. Now, at last, I can go forward at will, that is what I have gained from fear in all directions.

And the Director said:

"We should all be gravely at fault if we were to permit anyone to speak about his father as our colleague has spoken. Therefore, we can do no less than demand of him that he should turn again with his whole heart and mind to his father and, in that spirit, come to grips with his doubts.

Yes, indeed, there is an element of tragedy in this case! We are witnesses of a grave crisis experienced by one among us, and let us all take to heart the final warning: He who holds such views about his father's life-work is no true son, and the father who failed to respond by disowning his son, though he be his own son, would be no true father!"

"Friends," I said when I stood once more before them, "colleagues," I proclaimed ceremoniously. There was no time to think what I should say, I had only the minute or so allowed for my right of reply. And therefore, planted there in me, in place of any positive ideas, was just this ban I had imposed upon myself. I must never allow myself to offend anyone by arrogance. So I said: "Colleagues, comrades, you have reminded me of my duty to my father. I have long been aware of it. But nevertheless – I shall talk with my father again. Why not, since I have to? Since in any case not a single movement of a single finger do I make without him?"

Sweat ran from every pore in my body as the heat focused and drew me within its range. The path wound up to the steep slope of the clearing and there, from one end to the other, it crackled with the heat. The tall grass creaked, immobile, and a faint scent of ants and snakes lingered in the air above. I wondered what I would see if now, at high noon, I were able to soar over the countryside. In the shade of fir trees by the railroad, half-naked labourers sipping their beer, while over the picks they have left by the track, cabbage-whites are fluttering. Under the bushes in the meadows, sweating women co-operative farmers who have been tossing the hay and are themselves being helplessly tossed by society; on straw under their shelter, aged herdsmen drinking water out of beer bottles; factory workers who have taken time off to gather in fuel for the winter and are now resting their backs against their stacks of wood, and dozing. I alone am walking here – without purpose, purely for my own satisfaction do I engage in this minor torment which has no relevance whatsoever to my work, because my work requires instruments of a kind incomprehensible and useless in these parts. However did it come about! I moved away quite imperceptibly, day by day, and now I am a whole life removed. I return once a year and always I take this path. People try to dissuade me, it is terribly hot, they say, there is a storm brewing, they prophesy, and why ever do I go when there is no need, since I have no hay here, no cows here, and I am not felling timber here. So now I go without telling anyone that I am going – and going alone – simply because I want to go. You see, I know that when once I finally decide not to set out, I shall be old, and I shall bow to that knowledge. True, one summer I may lie down right here, and goodness knows how long it will be before they find me covered with ants. But, for the present, I'm not aware of any decline which could, or should, warn me that time is short. Only the thoughts . . . Why do they keep coming?

I stopped, not because I needed to rest, but because I had suddenly felt the touch of a forgotten moment and it brushed my face like spiders' webs on a long-untrodden path. I glanced around, hoping that the lie of the land, and the vegetation, despite its constant death and rebirth which I always take into account, would help me to locate a certain spot. I found it, I think, although today old scree gleams whitely on the lumber-slide, but my eyes erect above it the beech-clad hill where we used to roam through the rustling leaves. Dad would be continually disappearing in the grey, perpendicular-ruled forest, and when I drew near him he would chase me away. Because we were supposed to cover as wide an area as possible. But, in any case, I covered nothing at all, because I was so afraid of being alone that I was blind to the details of the ground on which I trod. I was watching all the time in case I might still catch a glimpse of him through the interweaving pillars of those twilit arches. A vast shadowy vault where an occasional jay uttered its shrill cry, and where the sun never shone. And when I had not seen Dad for a longish time, I stopped in terror, holding my breath to hear from which direction the leaves were rustling beneath his feet. When he had found something, he spoke. And I ran with the dry twigs crackling on my way. That Sunday, however, we had little enough to show: a few wood mushrooms, two or three blue ceps and some chantarelles. When Dad spoke, I raced towards him and he said: "See this big fellow?" He said this as he was stowing the big blue cep into his cherished brief-case, his eyes fixed on the mushroom as he did so and ... he stood transfixed, his mouth half open. Slowly he turned his head in the direction to which I am turning now. I stopped dead, a quarter of a century ago, and I listened, as he did, with all my strength; some minutes passed before I picked up in all the murmurous waves the faint dong, dong, dong ...

Noontide, people everywhere, a holiday, a gay world, all in their Sunday best, and we here, lifted out of time, and that gaping, shapeless, primeval-brown, cherished brief-case in his arrested hand. The deep-mouldering earth breathes upon us, white worms gnaw and corrupt the old blue cep, no sunshine penetrates the vault, and I see with amazement that Dad's hands, too, are drained of colour, I raise my eyes to his face – it is not there. And in these cruel circumstances I am to talk with him.

9

The conference over, I betook myself to the lavatory. I had no wish to meet anyone, not having prepared a way of approaching my colleagues following this event. Also I had an idea that the first move should come from them and that they should demonstrate our future mode of behaviour by means of some calculated action rather than a chance improvisation arising, for instance, from the technical circumstance of having to quit this building through the same hole. Naturally, I never imagined that anyone would seek me out here, of all places. More probably they would wait in the passage. Were I to leave at once, however, it could happen that someone would be standing there for an entirely different reason, he would see me and imagine that I thought he was waiting for me, and not wanting to disappoint me, he would behave in a manner he had not intended. Having followed this line of thought for a while, it struck me that, on the other hand, someone might actually be wanting to talk to me, might really be waiting for me, but being unable to wait for more than a reasonable time, when that time had passed he would start wondering and it would occur to him that I was intentionally spurning his opening move and avoiding our conversation, whereupon fear of a rebuff would cause him to leave sooner than he had intended. Was this the right way, on my part, to contrive the natural conception of our new relationship? Probably not; so I was doing precisely the opposite of what I desired. I hurried into the corridor. But there was nobody there.

Following my recent return from Girl's Town, while

still in the lift I had been indulging in similar worries about my first words on entering the office.

In the event: "Salaam aleykum," I said in greeting, as was my custom.

"Christ is risen," Slavek replied in ringing tones.

"To the Lord's table, gentlemen," came through the chief's door.

It is a long table, of walnut, covered by a slab of thick glass, and with the chief's desk it forms the letter T. Each of us sits, lies or props himself up in his accustomed place. I was fond of this room because of the many confidential words that had been spoken there, words which joined us in a warm protective huddle against the unpleasant blasts outside, and because I had never been subjected to any unfriendly attention there. Now that they were all together, I saw no particular reason to suppose that things had grown worse for me. I possessed, in a way, an initial advantage: for all of them, including our exasperated chief, were curious to know what the girl had been up to and what I had discovered in the town. When I had made my report, a colleague, a one-time member of the old communist *avant-garde*, remarked:

"Now that really is a story for a reportage. Kisch, write it up!"[1]

"That's just marvellous," the chief said, waving a match over his cigar to extinguish the flame. "And, what's more, I know the point of the story, which will round off the reportage and which even our Kisch here doesn't know yet – that they want to take him from us."

With a dramatic gesture, he picked up a scrap of paper and sent it down the line to me. It had been ascertained, I read, that in the past few days I had frequented such and such places and engaged in such and such talks. Since our editorial staff had no authority to engage in any talks

1 Referring to Egon Erwin Kisch, the Prague German writer (died 1948); known as "the roving reporter" for his colourful exploits as a journalist.

concerning the aforesaid matter, an explanation was required and strict measures were called for regarding my person.

"And time's flying," the chief announced, glancing at the neon clock where the minute figures were racing past the dial.

Whereupon everyone looked at the clock and at me. A sub-editor came in with page proofs and silently placed them before some of those present. They started reading.

"But I would still like to know," the chief continued, "what the present company expects of me in this situation. I may, perhaps, be allowed to ask that?"

They raised their heads.

"In ten minutes the Director wants to hear what I have to say, so excuse the haste."

Almost everyone whistled.

"Tell him we can't allow the regions to dictate to us."

"Thank you, I'll tell him that. Any more daft proposals?"

"Let him lick his arse," remarked the member of the prewar *avant-garde*.

"Try to explain to him that so far no one has really tried to establish the main thing – whether the girl's complaint was justified."

"Yes. I'll persuade him that the headmaster is an idiot and that a gang of rascals is running the district. That's an excellent idea. He'll be surprised!"

"Tell him that we just won't write about anything any more," I said.

"I'll tell him everything you've suggested," the chief assured us, "some time when I'm under the table with him."

Nobody could think of anything more. These were our established attitudes and our roles and our customary remarks.

"Primarily you undoubtedly want our colleague to remain among us," the chief said. "Therefore be so good as to listen to what I say. Our colleague did not of his own accord go to the deceased girl's town. Naturally, he went there because I sent him. I'm surprised you've forgotten that."

"Bravo," someone murmured.

"Pepik, you're great," Slavek told the chief.

The chief's cigar had gone out, and as he relit it, his thick lips curved in a circle like the Capek brothers'.[1]

"I cannot accept your words of praise," he continued, "because there is no question here of any magnanimity on my part; it was, as you will recall, the view of the Party group and I merely acted in accordance with that view."

We all looked at Slavek who, on hearing these words, had been seized with a fit of suppressed laughter. Today, knowing what happened later to Slavek, I have rediscovered our original happy relationship which evidently sprang from the circumstance that he had a high opinion of me, though he was a far better man than I, with greater depth, while also being more circumspect and modest. Therefore, when I think of him today it is as though the events I am describing here had been forgotten. It is the old friendship, with only a drop added to it from the bitter cup of experience, my experience.

Slavek rubbed his upper lip, chuckled shortly and said:

"What the comrade, our principal, says is correct. Having been accused of publishing an article which evoked certain consequences of a nature unknown to us, we were obliged to go ahead, that is, to complete our investigation of the case. And it was undoubtedly right that this task fell to the one among us who caused it all."

Unfortunately, in my joy at the way my friends had come to my aid, I failed to notice the little kick-back contained in Slavek's final sentence, that is, in the words *who caused it all.*

1 Karel Capek, author of *RUR, The Insect Play, War with the Newts,* and other books and plays, all well known in English translation, and his brother Josef Capek, painter and writer.

At this point the chief extinguished his cigar and departed.

When, half an hour later, he passed through our room, all I got from him was a grave, silent nod as he retreated into his study, where he immediately had the page proofs brought to him; he prudently threw out a commentary on educational reform, since it dealt, among other matters, with the all-round assessment of candidates for further education. However, this simple preventive measure of the chief's turned out badly: we had all forgotten that on the front page, already set up in type, was a notice about this article. Next day it proved quite impossible to persuade anyone that the outrageously elementary error was a mere oversight.

In this heated atmosphere we sat next day round the walnut table to debate no less a matter than when I was to be sacked. The Director of the Trust – according to the chief – had accepted the fact that I had made the second trip to Girl's Town, that having been the decision of the Party group. The error, in his view, lay elsewhere: in the fact that, by his unqualified support for the girl, the reporter had artificially counterposed her interests to the interests of society.

"That's old hat," we all said at this point.

The member of the prewar *avant-garde* beckoned to me across the table, he leant towards me, and I to him, and in a hoarse whisper he breathed in my face the opinion:

"It's the Stalin bureaucracy all over again," and when I nodded agreement, he continued: "But Trotsky was no alternative."

Though I hadn't a clue to what that meant, I thought it best to wave my hand with a knowing grin, as much as to say, we all know about that. Then I gave my full attention to most interesting words, like these:

"The Director does not wish us to have a reporter of this type on our staff."

Now they had been spoken, the long-awaited words

were, despite my efforts, as unpleasant as might have been expected. And at this moment our girl trainee, whose place was next to mine, emitted a quiet splutter, she doubled up and covered her mouth. Tugging at my sleeve, she pointed to a line of the freshly printed number that lay before each of us.

I looked closer and saw in our paper: "In times *long-pisst* an historic event . . ."

"Why are you playing the fool?" the chief asked crossly. Our reporter of six months was the only one of us not to use his first name, and he was also the last of us not to use hers.

"Please, sir, there's a double 's' in the wrong place," the trainee replied.

He frowned uncomprehendingly. I had to laugh.

"The bloody fool still has the cheek to laugh," Slavek said, and he laughed.

"And I think that's fine. Is he supposed to cry?" remarked the frivolous young person beside me.

"No," replied Slavek, "but he might perhaps take the trouble to consider with us how to get out of this mess."

She flapped her hand and murmured something which she was afraid to say out loud.

"What are you muttering again over there?" the chief grumbled wearily.

"That I'd like to go and shoot the Director."

I rose and went to the Director. I asked the secretary to send in my name. She did so and told me to wait for five minutes.

"Well, take a seat."

"I'd rather not, you're very kind."

She laughed, then went over to the drinks cupboard and poured me a vodka. I thanked her, I drank it and took a seat as she had wished.

One of her telephones rang, she lifted the receiver, glanced up and held the instrument towards me. I indicated that I did not wish to speak, and she said:

"He doesn't want to. And his name's been sent in already – he looks all right."

The next moment she knew by some signal that I was to go in.

He was sitting at the head of his big T, a bigger one than ours. When I had greeted him, he stood up and, waiting until I had marched towards him past the long row of chairs, he held out his hand. "I would have called you in any case," he said.

"I understand that the question whether the girl was in the right will never be investigated," I said as a beginning.

"That's not the real issue," he replied. "Suppose she *was* right – but you weren't!"

He almost smiled as he spoke, he was young, five years older than myself, if that. He was not at all hostile. This was my first encounter with him.

"I don't understand," I objected, "If she was right, then whoever takes her part must be right, too."

He considered, he laughed.

"Yes. But one has to know how to deal with the truth. If she was in the right, had the truth on her side . . . then why isn't she alive today?"

I saw, in all its catastrophic breadth, right under my nose, just the other side of his desk, the impossibility of any understanding between us, although he spoke Czech.

"I don't wish to continue my employment with you," I said.

"I have already put through the proposal," he replied.

"No, Comrade Director. I refuse to accept dismissal. I am giving notice to leave this firm."

"I don't believe that's possible. The grounds are on our side."

"Think again. If you sack me, I shall tell everyone how things were. I know lots of people in Prague, and I have about a hundred and fifty relatives in Moravia. You'll have the shock of your life!"

"What's that? Oh, yes. One must know how to deal with the truth. You don't know how to deal with it."

My colleagues were still sitting round the conference table, only – as certain signs told me – what had started as an editorial conference had turned, in my absence, into a political meeting: the chief was no longer in the chair, Slavek was there, and the chief had taken Slavek's place. The member of the *avant-garde* was sitting beside Slavek. Otherwise nothing had changed in the fifteen-headed gathering, just one proof reader had gone and a typist had come. When I arrived, they stopped talking and the Old Avantgardist said in an undertone to Slavek: "Tell him."

"Well, we've been considering it all," Slavek said, "and I think we're unanimous in not wanting to lose you. It would be a loss for the office."

"And for the paper," the Old Avantgardist prompted gently.

"And for the paper, of course," said Slavek and he continued: "If the worst is not to happen, we have to forestall it – I don't know if I'm putting this correctly – if not, please say so."

"You're saying it quite right," said someone and the chief.

"But there's no use thinking, for instance, that we can reject all criticism out of hand. That would probably be the end of us all, and I don't know, but I imagine you're concerned about the paper, too . . . or aren't you? You say . . ."

"But of course I am. So what's the idea?"

"Now, if we admit that some blame has been incurred, we shall then be in a position to insist that the thing isn't as serious as the management makes out and that, therefore, the conclusions they draw are out of all proportion, if you follow me . . ."

"Look here, my friend," the Old Avantgardist came to Slavek's aid, emitting the hoarse wheezing which signified his laughter, "if we take your case into our own hands, we can ward off a far worse eventuality. We'll say: excuse us, this is our affair, which we can put straight by ourselves – and we'll rap all of them over the knuckles. But of course we can only do that if we say that we've, you know, ourselves . . ." he scrawled with a bent, white finger over the thick, green glass, ". . . that we've punished you ourselves."

"Punished? What for!" our girl-trainee bounced beside me.

"You're our little girl," I said, and I stroked her hair.

On the other side of the table, the chief raised a hand.

"I would point out – to make sure we're not deluding ourselves. If we do admit some blame, let us not think to ourselves that we're merely going through the motions, as a tactic. That would be the greatest disservice we could render to our colleague!"

"What bla-a-ame?" our trainee twisted from left to right and from right to left.

"We all bear the blame. Given a better knowledge of the background, we could have published the very same article as the one we carried, and possibly a far sharper one."

"I can just see you signing my permit for the trip if I'd told you I was going out on a case in which a headmaster and half the district were involved!"

"I protest! That kind of case developed after your article!"

"So there! So there!" I crowed. "So now tell me, anybody, what you find wrong in that article today."

Silence.

"My dear fellow," Chairman Slavek addressed me calmly, "you amaze me. Are you really, in your own mind, so sure? Why, after your article – the girl died!"

I hurried into the corridor, but there was nobody there. Who should have been there, anyhow, and the trainee wouldn't, after all, be standing in front of the gents' toilets. Smoke drifted from the empty conference chamber and the staff were gathering up the tablecloths and putting the tables back in their original order. I retreated down the deserted stairway to the street, and I discovered that it was dark outside. Cars were passing quietly and the blue light of street lamps was shining through the maple leaves in the park. Moreover, everything around me seemed to be swaying; I knew it all depended on me, I had only to comply. I did not comply and I walked slowly past the house-fronts. What astonished me most was how by word, mere word, things can change their proportions and a man's position among them changes, too. By the force of mere words even new things can emerge, and to accept that is to live in a world of phantoms. But he who rejects it finds himself faced by another disquieting set of earlier phantoms, and these have either to be covered up again, or it is necessary to delve into the deeper layers . . . how many are piled there one upon another? When do we finally reach the genuine things, the things of wood, leather, stone or iron? Did the mistake lie in my visiting Girl's Town? Ach! Then, was it that I joined this firm? In that case, I should never have entered this profession. But then, of course, I need not have studied, but then, there was no need for me to leave home, but then . . . no, I'll not repeat it, anyhow it is hopeless to try explaining to anyone, what's done is done, I have told all and amazed everyone. Undoubtedly, they were capable of comprehending anything under the sun – in a metaphorical sense. Or as an extravagance, a leg-pull, a rag, a brainstorm, or as a daring analogy. But no, they were incapable of grasping that when speaking at the conference I had reached matters of wood, leather, stone or iron. One man alone understood, the man who was meant to understand, the man I had addressed and in whose person I had been addressing them all – the Director. And he, too, responded correctly and precisely, he alone.

In my stomach, where I should have felt hunger, there

was sand. I could no longer exist by any process of thought, but solely by my sensory perceptions, like a dog. There goes a car, there go people, neon shines above an hotel, on the opposite side of the road it is dark. It was a mood to which a character in a modern novel would have responded in the grand manner: he would have had a drink of some sort, made a phone call to some place, taken a taxi and driven off somewhere, home maybe, where he might fling a few things into a suitcase and let some night express or other bear him north or south.

"Wherever have you been?" Slavek asked. "I've been waiting for you . . ." He stepped from the shade of a tree into the street lighting.

"I was delayed," I said.

"Yes, I saw you'd gone to the loo. You vomited there?"

"Well, not exactly . . ."

"But you almost did, didn't you?"

For a few minutes we walked in silence. We turned into the park. The flower-beds were ablaze with tulips, but in the dark, and that induced in me a mood that things are as they are. Whether we know or not. Just as there is no reason to grieve over something unknown to us, there is, of course, no reason to rejoice when we learn about it.

"My first idea, back there in the hall," Slavek broke the silence, "was that you'd simply gone off your head. Then, you know, a dreadful suspicion came over me that you're terribly strong and I'm a lousy coward and that everything I've been doing over the past weeks has been dictated by my cowardice plus my urge to hide it."

He stopped and I said nothing. What was there to say, anyhow?

"And while I've been waiting for you here, I've had another thought. You're an outright individualist and egoist. But not in the vulgar sense, the term of abuse some people use, but in a far worse sense, bordering on the absolute. You see, you're an exceedingly self-sacrificing egoist and an individualist capable of putting your head in the noose."

"And what does that mean?" I couldn't manage to keep silent any longer.

"It means enormous pride and almost. inhuman arrogance. God has to punish you, the Party expel you, egoists hate you and individualists have to feel their freedom threatened by you."

"This makes me feel quite good, just carry on."

"You want to be the purest of the pure, but why! Are you better than other people, in a class apart? Who do you suppose you are, anyhow? Why should you achieve something that nobody's got?"

"You're right, and you're not right. What you accuse me of wanting isn't anything impossible. I can't help it if it's regarded more and more as a luxury. Actually it's no more than a primitive response to impulses from the environment."

"Yes, but so you can respond primitively to impulses from the environment you involve more and more people. It gets me down," Slavek said.

"Those who come to terms with the facts will survive," the psychiatrist from the hospital told him, and since the psychiatrist was not present, I spoke for him.

"Tell me," Slavek asked, "do you regard the things people are doing outside the gates of your madhouse as a coming to terms with the facts, or as giving shape to these awful facts?"

"Sir," the doctor replied, "I believe in viewing matters squarely and I am a dialectician, so I say – they are doing both! Whoever is afflicted by the facts is ready to acknowledge their existence, which is the best thing he can do. But he who is creating these facts is not yet ready to take cognizance of them. By his deeds he reaches outwards, he feels no inner pain and there is no point in bringing it home to him and saying: 'All in good time!' "

We were making our second round of the park, meeting

a few solitary figures, and as we passed them we stopped talking. After a long pause, Slavek said:

"You have a pretty poor opinion of me now, haven't you?"

"I'm simply of the opinion that you're working against me. In any case."

"And that I'm trying to save you from the Director, you don't see that?"

"Are you daft, or what? That was just what he needed – our self-governing terrorizing of ourselves!"

Slavek said nothing. I realized that I had succeeded for the first time in expressing something so perfectly. But it had taken years!

"Actually, that's what the Czech invention amounts to – terrorizing ourselves so democratically that there's no one for us to assassinate."

Slavek burst out laughing, quietly and breathlessly.

"You've said it, mate!" he brought out jerkily, shaking his head appreciatively, "it's almost a definition of history!"

I said nothing to that. What was there to say, since it was a definition?

"But in that case you ought to admit," Slavek said, "that any kind of rebellion is useless. Look: all attempts to criticize social systems have had just one result, that the systems have adapted themselves, and they have also evolved for themselves a wider immunity so that their control of people simply grows more and more elaborate and ingenious. Leaving barely a chink for escape."

"Yes," I said. "But by telling me that you're actually sealing up another chink for me, aren't you? Do you know what? The best thing is not to speak to anyone."

"You might have thought of that sooner," Slavek remarked coldly.

Today, knowing what happened later to Slavek, I cannot swear that our conversation was exactly as I have written it here. It strikes me as scarcely possible that our argument could have shaped so clearly and comprehensively. More probably we groped for ways of formulating our ideas, with effort worthy of more pleasant matters. For if we had really told each other so clearly the things I know today, we would both, in fact, have seen beforehand what we were heading for, and so we would have known everything, everything, including what was in store for Slavek.

"I wouldn't like to prophesy," Slavek continued, shifting to his other hand the heavy briefcase in which he was always carrying heavy books to and fro between his home and the office, "but I'm afraid the account you gave today about your dad's life and work will have achieved just one result: they'll consider it necessary to work out a definition establishing the correct nature of fatherhood and sonhood. Are you with me?"

"I am!" I was so stunned that I stopped in my tracks. They would take yet another area of human relationships under their idiotic jurisdiction! I understood only too well. They would set up a commission. They would send us its findings to publish in the paper. We would print approving letters, and they would be genuine letters, from tangible fatheads!

"Slavek, I must go home immediately!"

"Worst of all," he replied, "is when you're not sure whether you're a coward or not."

He was always worrying in those days about being cowardly.

"I'm going home immediately," I repeated, "but I'll tell you one more thing, there was a time when I used to worry myself about whether philosophizing isn't merely the refuge of people who lack muscle. So long."

"I suppose there hasn't been a war, or a conflagration for quite a time," Slavek said, going ahead and forcing me to follow a pace behind him. "Don't go home. And that's what has led to the degeneration of virtues – there hasn't been anything for a long time now."

"Just think," I said to him, "how silly you'll look if, in fact, there's no cause either for courage or for fear. Suppose we've been imagining all these dangers?"

He halted, shifted his heavy briefcase and said: "What's that you're saying?"

"That perhaps it's all hysteria on our part, and actually nobody is threatening us."

After a moment's consideration, he replied:

"And do you know that it doesn't matter? It doesn't matter whether outside, apart from us, there are genuine causes for courage or for fear, or whether we have simply imagined them. Because whichever way it is, you have to tackle the question and you suffer just the same." Thus spoke Slavek and sadly he came to a standstill.

It was a remarkable ramification of our problem. Man, a being endowed with a conscious capacity for fear and for courage, emerged from the hunting grounds and the wars on to the clear plain, and failing to see the familiar dangers, he was afraid that his cowardice was conjuring up a rosy vision. He attacked. Against whom?

"So long, Slavek!"

What if it is so! What if in reality there's nothing wrong? For, as it would appear, he who wants nothing, lacks nothing! Perhaps *it* simply doesn't exist, perhaps I have created it myself? I walked past a bar where I didn't stop for a drink, I made a point of going into the railway station to examine the departure indicators. Wherever could I go. South to Budejovice – but it's just the same there! North to Dechin – I'd be there in a couple of hours and at journey's end, without having got away. In all directions it is the same, the same bread, the same organizations and horrible chlorinated water runs from the taps in the hotel room. Equally healthy everywhere and no ghostly apparitions lurking anywhere over the marshes. Moreover, I haven't the money for a train, nor for a hotel, and if I had a drink at the bar now, I would have to go for a week without a drink in the canteen. I am left with my honour and a journey home on foot. I am a low-paid worker.

I laughed. That's it, I am a low-paid worker! So I am a low-paid worker and it all stems from that. Good grief, that's how the ordinary, normal man sees it – as a matter of what can be attained. Really, it's marvellous, sssh! they mustn't hear, or they'd give us more money, and be rid of us . . .

"Actually, I'm a low-paid worker," I said as I opened the front door and my startled wife appeared in the doorway opposite.

"What's wrong?" she asked.

"I'm underpaid, that's what it boils down to. But nobody must know."

She went in again and through the open door she said:

"Don't worry, they won't get to know."

The children were asleep. It occurred to me that there could be much worse things, really bad things: a wall and a fence might come between me and my wife, and I would have nobody to talk to, perhaps never again. I was in a hurry to make the most of the circumstance that in the meantime there really wasn't anything wrong, and I said:

"Do you take care of yourself? If not, there's no guarantee that nothing will happen to you."

"No fear about me! What about you, do you take care? Very little effort is required to bring downright misfortune upon oneself."

"You're wrong there," I turned on the cold tap for a drink of water as I spoke, "no effort at all! It's enough to act in accordance with the logic of events, or to reply to questions. Where are you going – that's none of your business. Do you want – no I don't. And so on."

Over tea with bread and redcurrant jam we agreed that there is no social mechanism, anywhere in the world, capable of separating man from his possible misfortune. On the contrary, it is as though everything was just waiting to oblige the citizen should he give the slightest sign of wanting to be destroyed. Mr Prime Minister, you are a rascal. Sir, the Prime Minister replies, I am prohibited from taking note of any statements from you which might do you an injury – I apologize, Mr Prime Minister! Indeed, it occurs to me now that I must have been mistaken. "Where is there such a country?" I asked myself.

"History has no meaning, I realized that long ago," my wife replied.

In peace and quiet we went to bed, and no one stopped us. If I took things out of my pockets, I could put them wherever I wished. And I noted with satisfaction that I felt no longing for the great cities, that, on the contrary, they left me pretty cold; in fact, they are the image of that hysteria which with bestial howls is butting in on us, disrupting and rending as it goes. I sensed – in the presence of my wife – that a world like that would, in any case, never accept me, thereby facilitating my decision that I, for my part, would never wish to accept it, that even the attempt to do so would be misplaced. Return and start again. When they begin examining (is it possible?) whether I am any kind of a son at all, I have to know whose, and I must not force myself into an image which is not mine by right. Therefore I have to seek within myself the entelechy – no more suitable terms occurs to me – that has been reposed in me, if my entire life is not to prove an error and my death no more than an embarrassing let-out for those close friends who may have taken me seriously.

As I slept I dreamt of the hills, which were slowly turning all their sides to me, and I could see the familiar slopes and gullies, strangely mingling, however, with the unknown and unsuspected, I walked towards them and I found myself in unexpected places and there was no end to the recognizing and discovering because these hills were shifting all the time, at once intimately known and terrifyingly strange. And miracles took place: lady's slipper blossomed in the meadows beside autumn crocus, violets with moon daisies, and by mere will I could rise above the maples to seek what I would in the valleys below.

This is the spot where, last time we were here, we encountered a noble viper. And here I should have been able to hear the blows of the axe. I stood still. At first not a sound, and that scared me. Curbing my panic, however, I reminded myself that I must patiently unravel the grey murmuring around me down to its fibres. And true enough, in a while I detected the delicate knots in the woodland quiet. Setting my course by them, I soon heard the rhythmic hacking blows which sounded like a creaking cough. Then, when Dad came into view, I realized that it really was his chronic bronchial cough, while the strokes of the broad-axe were softer, fading to a finer end. Two, three blows, two, three coughs, that was the truth of it.

"Welcome, son. So you've come?"

A strong scent of resin came from the spot where he stood.

"I've brought your dinner, Dad."

"And what's our Mother doing?"

"She's gone to hoe the potatoes."

"And what is our lassie doing?"

"She's rocking the baby and boo-hooing the while."

I was referring to my driver brother, the one I am supposed to be visiting for the first time, although my run-up to the story is pretty odd, in all conscience!

"Why is she boo-hooing?" Dad inquired.

"She doesn't want to rock him."

"Blast!" said Dad, and he embedded his axe in the wood, stepped over the tree trunk and took the bag of food from me.

"You've had your dinner?"

"Yes, but a long time ago."

When we had finished eating, we were thirsty and the black rye-coffee I had brought was not enough for us.

"Will you go for water?" he asked me. He pointed to the east. "Run over that way about six hundred yards. You'll find a spring – there's a big stone screening it. But don't use the can, you'd muddy the water. On the stone there'll be an earthenware mug."

I ran down into the deep, dry gulley where the leaves lay knee-deep. Afraid of losing the direction, I forced a path straight through the bushes. Then I crossed level ground, in the wood all the time, until I dropped into a deep gulley. Trees sprouted horizontally from the sheer banks before twisting up towards the sky. A short walk against the stream brought me to the spring. A mossy stone screened it. I picked up the mug with its handle missing and the rim chipped almost jagged. Newts took fright in the water.

Dad rinsed his mouth without drinking. His dry complexion shone faintly.

"Was it there?"

"What?"

"The mug. A brown one."

"Yes, brown, with the handle gone."

He embedded the axe within a hair's breadth of the line marked out on the stripped trunk. And before making the prising movement to tear off a chip of wood, he let go of the haft, spat on his palms. and thoughtfully rubbed them together.

"Hm, I can tell you exactly. The last time I drank out of it, that'll be twenty years. But it was there before then, before I went to the war. Just the same, except it had a handle. I used to graze the cows at the foot of that hill."

The going was better now among the spruces, though to my mind a spruce wood is a gloomy place to pass through. Stopping to take off my rucksack, I made sure that the axe had not shifted to a position where it might cut the fabric. Since I was carrying my jacket, I now used it to wrap the axe head. In these woods almost nothing grew.

Walking through a spruce wood does not appeal to me, because it is dead. Only grey stones break through the thick, springy carpet of needles. To me it suggests a secret graveyard of something, of a genuine wood perhaps. Over the hills and dales, in the deep dark woods, there lies a grave ringed about with flowers – when Mother used to sing that song it was a wood like this that always came naturally to my mind. My chief aversion is for the northern slopes of conifer-covered hills, and forebodings of evil visit me when I pass that way. My estimation of the western slopes is similar, whereas to the south and to the east it is quite different. In short, I am afraid, and the inclination to drop down into the beech woods some six hundred yards to the east is growing on me now.

The strong pull of iron in the blood draws me there and who knows where it might land me. Would I be able to hold it from rejoining its original bed? To the man who is now in my thoughts, water was water, and a tree a tree. He was a man in the woods, here's water, we'll quench our thirst. But can I, as the light is dawning upon me, can I pretend that I know nothing?

Water for the wells in the village gathered in this wooded upland basin, and he drank it. It was transfused through the grasses into the udders of the cows. It shaped itself as fruit, and that fruit he ate. Here is a deposit of the matter from which came the atoms that assembled in his body. Ah, why did they pass and repass here so often, with a step as ominous and heavy in the end as the tread of an elephant trekking to the graveyard of elephants! And how am I to find an explanation for my need to come here over and over again, never missing a year, and if I do miss, I am almost ill? How can I go against my own self?

It occurs to me that I have put many questions to

people, but there is one question I have never yet thought of asking:

"Where, actually, do you come from in terms of your atoms?"

And they will hunt around until they discover a siding where railway waggons are reloaded, and they will find no other reports about themselves. Because the potatoes composing their souls could have come from the Highlands, the phosphorus for their bones from one of the oceans. Their whole being comes from consignments of raw materials, instead of from this or that valley. Terrible, wherever can I find a point of contact there? Better not to ask them, but presumably they love their freight yards and their native slag heaps. And since these places are subject to change, indeed it is desirable to change them, these people have embraced the principle of change and they apply it catastrophically to the hills and vales as well, and that misapprehension really could drive one to murder. I am beginning to doubt whether communication with these people is really what I want. With synthetic men there can be no communication.

I walked on through the dark woods. I have no liking for the northern and western slopes, that I have known very well for a long time now. I have been around in the world long enough, and I am surprised to find that my first impression of this world was correct. When I was born, I mounted a hill and surveyed the scene. And it struck me at once that in the direction of Moravia and Bohemia I observed nothing that boded any good. That's the truth, even as a boy I had the idea that there was absolutely nothing over there for me to dream about. Today I am discovering the truth of that. For the people themselves lack the stuff of dreams. My childhood instinct was correct. One should not be so anxious to discover what people elsewhere possess and what they are doing. One should not be continually comparing oneself with others and always reckoning the disparities to one's disadvantage. And why struggle so hard to keep up with this or that when, for the most part, it's heading for the arse-hole.

And therefore: ape America if you want, you Czech copy-cat!

Because: what have you to offer, anyhow, you monopolistic numbskulls?

10

Unlike the conference, the woods are peaceful and pleasant. The dream is coming true. I walk in the woods as in a dream and the time is drawing near when, by a manifest act, I shall consummate my secret decision. The act is profanely tempting, and though one might suppose I could still back out, that is not so. No man is ever the same after rejecting an idea that has entered his head as he was before it entered his head. The act which I am now approaching has begun to look a bit different: it is dangerously within range, I shall go through with it, and soon I shall know what it *looks* like from the other side. How shall I *feel*? Then I shall go away and, according to my calculations, it will be impossible for me to slip back into the old rut. The road to the accursed spiritual morasses where men do nothing but wonder who they are, whether they may do what they wish, what they would lose if – what would be done to them if – that road to the quagmires of doubting about the right to doubt – that road ought then to be blocked to me.

However, before describing how I journeyed to my brother the driver and what I did there, I need to explain rather more about our beautiful house and about Dad, who said:

"There are certain questions concerning the ordering of our domestic affairs in the event of unforeseen circumstances."

"I'm not capable even of thinking about that," I replied.

This dialogue always took place in the last few minutes

before my train, when it was impossible to say anything whatsoever. I was doubly dispirited – by what he persisted in wanting to discuss, and by the fact that once more, with the passage of time, we had failed to talk about it.

At first I couldn't even understand what he really had in mind. When it dawned on me, I was shocked. He was actually speaking about death, his own and Mother's, as though it were something that had to come one day. No, I simply was not ripe for anything like that. And yet, later, I would sometimes be startled to find myself trying to imagine the manner of these deaths and reflecting about who would be first.

I said nothing, I got into the train and it carried me away into the black tunnel where, in the mechanical, raw rumbling darkness I toiled towards an acceptance of the facts.

And again I journeyed home, the floorboards were freshly scrubbed, behind the glass doors of the kitchen dresser a plate of cakes; and from the faces I tried to read the events which had occurred under this roof. I always liked to indulge myself by deciding that things had not been so bad. Good nights were said, alarm clocks wound up, a pan of water cooled on the stove, and they went into the other room, but in a while he returned to the kitchen where I used to sleep on the ottoman, making out that he had come for a cigarette, which he lit, then he adjusted the opening of his underpants, seated himself under the window and cleared his throat.

"Regarding the problem on which I touched last time, we still have to talk about that problem."

Problem, broblem, br, br – has that gone for ever for the children in our family? I am dreadfully big now, and it will get worse! I said nothing, and consequently the talk about the ordering of affairs in our home never took place, although appearances might have suggested otherwise. At the most I uttered some words, without, however meaning what I said. It was at this time that I first registered Mother's peculiar wisdom; she had no wish to solve any problems, she simply pulsated, knowing beforehand what was to come.

He took agonizing pains that I should be with him and should talk to him. Frequently it would happen that he had to walk around the village on some business. Three times he rose to go, fetched his coat and waited. I stood my ground. I stood my ground against the violence he was doing me by not speaking out, by waiting until my nerve broke and in the end I said:

"You're going out? I could go with you."

He was almost dancing with agitation, girding his coat with such vigour that one might have thought we were going into battle. Delight darted secretly beneath the tough, furrowed skin, but immediately he was gloomily concerned:

"If you really want to, by all means! But can you tear yourself away for a while?"

I was furious. Since all I had to do was to tear my bottom off the chair. The misery of devotion, the misery of subjection. We strode with grave demeanour along the street and out of the village, because he had postponed or cancelled his business, or, as it seems to me now, he probably had no business. He wanted me to tell him about my studies, about my friends, about Prague. And he made no comment, asked no questions, and who knows whether he listened, because out of the blue he announced: "We are living in historic times."

To that there was no answer, therefore I was silent.

"But dammit, what's going to happen now?" he said and we strode on. Birds flew away before us.

And all the time he wanted to discuss something fundamental. The fond wish of this ageing man was that his eldest son should want his cottage. And I was incapable of uttering a word. The word.

I had seen that house grow from its foundations and,

led by the hand, I had toddled every Sunday after dinner to look at the unfinished shell of brickwork. And there was a blinding sunny frost outdoors that time when I sat reading fairy tales while Dad was laying the last floorboards in the room. Until then we had lived in the kitchen, that is to say, between finishing the construction and the full occupation of the cottage I had started school and had sufficiently mastered the art of reading to be able to read about the Grand Vizier. That house was a terribly long time building! By the time it was completed, it was old. Brutality.

To this day the roof beams of that cottage bear the marks traced on them according to the steel joiner's square as they lay on the grassy patch behind the barn, but none of that is true any more, not even the barn. It is ourselves we love in things, our parents, or our wife. And just as it is true that old things have to go, it is true that I must fear the calm insensibility which, in clearing them away, justifies its harshness by proclaiming that go they must.

Anyhow, the time came when I discovered that Dad had completely forgotten about dying. We, that is, I, my sister and my wife, received a lesson about such a man when we began to imagine him as a grandad with grandchildren at his knee. He couldn't understand what we were talking about. This time *he* couldn't understand. Since I knew that I had to do with a man who, when roaming the countryside, had been in the habit of pruning, anonymously, other men's trees because he could not bear to see them neglected and suffocated, I spoke as follows:

"It is necessary to arrange matters," that was now the most appropriate tone to adopt, "it is necessary to arrange matters, Dad, with a view to your being able to devote yourself rather more amply to the garden."

"That has already occurred to me," he replied. "I am finding this war in Korea extremely tiring, our prime task is to bring that matter to a conclusion," he said with a full sense of responsibility towards his grandchildren.

For the hard truth about the evolution of the spirit is that one day a man sees his last chance. He mounts it, and at a wild gallop he tries to catch up with absolutely everything. Dad's last fiery steed was Party work. And you, friends, do you realize that your entire life is an ever more precise definition of what you will never be?

When I had won my wife and I brought her home for approval, Mother adopted a cautious attitude towards her, whereas Dad showed a courteous, almost man-of-the-world gallantry, with a tendency towards quick friendship. With Mother the relationship grew gradually and predictably closer, whereas his veered from one extreme to the other: from an ardent comradeship to an unjustified harshness. In short, he could never quite come to terms with her being my wife, not his. And so I have recourse to this analogy that one day a man sees his last chance – would that I may understand myself correctly when my time comes!

I came out of the spruce wood and there, right at my feet, the blue-green meadow plunged into the depths, and when I halted in stunned amazement, it hissed softly in my face. Its maw breathed cold. And behind me, the dark wood faintly rumbled in the still air. With every minute that passed the grey stones among its roots were slowly disintegrating. It was unbelievable that these dark happenings should be enacted in broad daylight beneath a blue July sky. I was standing here above a place I feared. The reason is unknown to me. Perhaps it isn't mine at all, perhaps Mother had it. Or Grandad, whose grandad was, perhaps, struck dead here by lightning at the gipsy's. Or maybe from this very spot, hidden in a load of hay, the first black roosters of our clan stealthily gained admittance to the barn, and there was no dislodging them. While I may laugh at these tales and hold firmly to the realm of probable fact, it is always possible, none the less, that here the Kumans may have cut off the heads of all my relatives, but for one girl who fled in terror from her violators and ever since – well, how do I know?

The truth is that we never ventured into the meadow from that path by the spruce wood.

"Mother was always afraid here," he said, but he offered no explanation.

"Dad, let's get away from here," she begged, and they went, and to be sure, they are not here.

I moved along the wood's edge. I have always wondered at the quantity of small stones piled up there to form a long mound between the meadow and the wood. What men can have carried them there and why? They can't have gathered them on the meadow and humped them uphill to the fringe of the wood! They would hardly have picked them up in the wood! How often have I puzzled stupidly over this, until today I have hit upon a simple explanation: here, where the wood is now, were fields. Heavens, how long ago it must have been that no one knows of it any more and this old wood is growing on the stumps of a yet older wood! And now I could see that they were fields of oats or millet, stony fields, high and wind-swept, bleak acres worked by a woman in a black jerkin with a white kerchief, extinct acres. With relief and a touch of malice, I reflected that things are not really so bad. What people are incapable of maintaining, the forest takes back unto itself.

They walked on together – before they were married, they would have been carrying a jug for raspberries – and they vanished from my sight among the trees. I am rather surprised that I can follow their movement so well, although there is, as yet, no reason for my existence. The explanation is simple, however: later, I existed! Everything is equally in the past: the days when they walked with the jug, the days when I came here with my father and he recalled her strange fear, and the days when my father walked here with my wife. And therefore, all times being equally in the past, the distinction between them has lost all meaning. Having stored themselves in a heap within me – if only they could have arranged themselves in chronological layers – they have undoubtedly combined and reacted together, it will be far simpler and inconceivably more logical to say straight out that I have always been here. And always, even when I am not to be seen, I shall be here. I, neighbour to the stones, conversing with my particles. And in that there is solace and the germ of happiness at the sorrows of the world, is there not?

We walked on, all four of us, and all five, six and seven, for part of my resolve is that next time I shall come here with my son, the first, second and others, that they, too, may possess this; we walked on and vanished among the trees, when suddenly.

When suddenly the woodland swerved to the side, wavered and toppled into the dale. From left to right, from west to east, empty space unfolded before us, as long-drawn-out and remote as the most resonant echo, swaying beneath the burden of light from the universe and shaking a harshly jangling cow bell. Across the far slope, mowers were advancing in line and they were mowing the grass beneath the snow, none had yet set foot in the heavy dew, and distant wains wide-laden with hay were meandering there unheard.

"It's lovely here." The girl's voice was hushed, and she was unaware that she would be my mother.

He had expected that. He had known that this would be the response after the gloomy journey over the spruce hill. I, too, expected it, but my wife exclaimed in surprise:

"I was here, at this lovely place, with your Dad last year!"

"You were here?" I said with disappointment.

"And it suited me excellently that I had an opportunity and a reason to talk about you," she continued.

"While you were away in the army, I needed at least to talk to someone about you all the time. It was stupid of me. Maybe it offended and hurt him."

The curved spine of the hill dipped gently beneath our feet, to the right the view opened ever wider towards the Slovak border, no great distance over an arm of the airy lake, and beyond the grand, flowing range of the forward skyline one sensed the promise of a further boundless expanse, and there, rising from the vaporous depths, towered the sombre mass of solid earth. On the other hand, about the pettifogging little hills huffily bunched to the left – that is, the west – there is nothing to be said.

The land disposed itself in unexpected planes, swelling and folding, and recounting in silent gesture the mighty primeval stirrings in the crust. As though by design, from the northern side fir woods mounted calmly to this place. Here, at the high crossroads of the winds, is the spot where they stood, we stood and I shall stand.

"Remember this place, my boy," he said, and I could not understand, although, today, the place speaks for itself.

They seated themselves under a mighty tree.

"Sit down," I said thirty-five years later.

"This is the very spot where your dad and I sat," she said, and she bent her head.

Suddenly I noticed that I was alone, I took off my haversack, leant against the tree and stretched my legs. Although you may tell yourself a hundred times that you are prepared, in the end you find you are not.

What Slavek and I had considered as a possibility so grotesque that it was almost beyond imagining, had appeared as a perfectly serious point on the agenda. Why I ever doubted, I just don't know. For everything is possible. The idea ought never to have entered our heads, because what enters one man's head, the next man will put into practice. Once it must merely have occurred to someone that wallets could be made from human skin, later, others did it. Should it occur to me today that I might cut the sun into two halves and shift one to the right, the other to the left, then I have decided that one day some will do just that. It is all a matter of technique and the appropriate organization. The only remedy – to stop the brain in time.

"We have to form an opinion as to whether it is possible for our colleague to be his father's son," the Chairman announced in deliberate, almost muted tones.

It can't be true, surely it can't be true! But it was! Slavek knew it, and he had foretold it, meaning that he was to blame for it.

"It appears, my friends, that the definition applied hitherto to this type of relationship will, in future, prove inadequate for our society," the Chairman continued.

"And why?" I asked.

There was a slight stirring of the torsos filled with the week-day lunch.

"The old-established concept of fatherhood stemming from the principle of the pendulum is mechanistic."

A thought occurred to me, but no sound escaped me.

"According to that concept we find absolutely anyone can be the son of his father. That does not correspond to the exacting demands we place today on the relationship."

"Do you place them, do you?" I nudged Slavek with my elbow, but he drew away.

The firm's lawyer took the floor, saying:

"The truth is, of course, that people are still influenced by the concept of the filial relationship deriving from natural law. The terminology might suggest that this concept of the relationship between father and son was an expression of complete freedom, for it implied that all without distinction were fathers and sons. However," and at this juncture the speaker pressed down the tobacco in the bowl of his pipe and relit it, "in its consequences the concept signified the utter enslavement of the personality, for whoever was once born to a father was the son of that father, come what might. There was absolutely nothing to be done about it, even when a father discovered that his son was not as he had envisaged him and, had he been able to decide, he would never have acknowledged him as a son."

I took the floor and objected:

"Our lawyer colleague has spoken to us as idiotically as his appearance would lead one to expect."

They laughed.

"You're crazy," Slavek whispered. "You're making it impossible for anyone to take your side."

". . . and society alone, in the interests of society, is entitled to decide where the relationship of fatherhood has actually been established and whether it remains valid," the Chairman concluded.

"Excuse me," I said, "am I to understand that you have no intention of discussing what I actually said at the conference about my father's life and work?"

They glanced at each other. The Chairman laughed and the man from Head Office, who was sitting next to him, indicated by an almost imperceptible gesture his desire to speak. An elderly man, with the complexion of a road-mender.

"Look you here, my friend," he addressed himself to me, holding out his hand, "you had a right to say what you did. In this country anyone can say what they think, that's so, isn't it?" He turned to the company. "But look, you yourse-e-elf, see here, you yourself were unhappy about your dad's work and you turned against it. Well, and for our part, it would be only right that you shouldn't be held responsible for your father, then there'd be no need for you to feel embarrassed among us and in our company, if you could say that after all he's not your old man, your dad, you know."

"But he is my father, road-mender!"

"Then what do you want?" asked a voice.

"No, no, wait a minute," I heard, and it was our chief. "Friends, to my mind ours is no easy role. True, the times reveal many new aspects of things and relationships. And an insensitive move can do more harm than good. Who among us can say that he has not forgotten any of the delicate intricacies of the relationship between father and son? I can well understand our colleague here. You know, he has two sides to him: profound sincerity, and verve, genuine verve. So at times he may slip up. Why, until now, none of us have put to ourselves in such sharp terms the question of following in the footsteps of our fathers! Can we, then, expect him not to put a foot wrong? We cannot. Especially when we are moving over uncharted ground. What we lack is the law. I am not referring to moral justification, our conscience is undoubtedly well founded in that respect, but it is the legal norm that we really lack."

I looked at Slavek, it was as clear as daylight, it was all working out for us as surely as it did for that Christmas virgin, as our Grandad used to say.

"I think," the chief continued, "that we should simply take note of this case, but refrain from drawing any hasty conclusions. Perhaps more competent bodies, endowed with legislative power, will view it as an impulse towards examining and defining that new reality on the brink of which we one and all find ourselves today."

This standpoint won the day, it was recorded in the minutes and within a month our chief was dismissed as unreliable.

I heard a heavy, shuffling tread in the grass, I lifted my head. A woman was passing. Still young, but haggard. She wore a red apron over the brown trousers of a track suit. She glanced briefly at me as she passed, and tramped on swiftly like someone hurrying to the opposite side of the valley to thrash a child.

Day in day out I was among people in the office who knew that the chief had been dismissed because of me. It could not have been made more palpably obvious that I was regarded as an irresponsible element. I was shaken, but no longer to the foundations. And then came the farewell party. During the month of waiting for the chief's departure all the circumstances had been debated everywhere so exhaustively that the party turned into one of those friendly evenings that can be held on any pretext. In any case, the chief was not being thrown out on his neck, as would have happened in the old days of capitalism, he was simply transferring to an equivalent post in another concern. He had received a second vote of confidence. Nevertheless, I had not anticipated such a free-and-easy, truly friendly atmosphere that evening. It took me some time to pluck up the courage to shed, bit by bit, as the hours passed, the convulsive sense of my own uncleanliness. After the third glass I began to think that I understood. Fact – nobody was inclined to be angry with me. I was absolutely sure about that from the moment when both the Director and the road-mender entered our room, both accepted drinks from the chief, they toasted him and wished him well in his new job.

"Well now, our revolutionary," the road-mender grinned at me over his wine.

Whereupon I realized that, in fact, people have for a long time now been viewing their position in the same fatalistic light as, say, the rim of a wheel turned by a pair of oxen must view itself. All that is required is for a man to accept a role, and also to show his colour honestly to his fellow players, then, once they have him placed, he is free to carry on in any manner within his role. Yes, I realized that I had been cast in the role of the unsackable firebrand, I was, so to speak, our regimental mascot whose private parts it was permissible to show on the screen, just as the chief was an interchangeable chief and the road-mender a normalized state idiot.

At one moment during the evening Slavek came up to me.

"Hi," he said. Then he flapped a hand. "Another time."

Amidst the hum of voices and the snatches of song and the ringing of the telephone from the compositors' room, somewhere there fluttered an elusive idea. It had no shape, nor did I even know what it was about. I struggled to grasp it, but I seemed to be in the borderland between dreaming and wakefulness – the idea appeared marvellous to me, and then, when I made to bring it forth from the twilight of semi-consciousness, it changed in my grasp into an endearing nonsense. And as I watched the distortion of my idea beneath the swirl of blurring waters, I decided I might try recording its ground-plan under water. And then we would see on dry land. Och, wasn't I drunk? What with? Maybe a wee dram. And to fit the way I saw the ground-plan of the idea, I traced a cross to serve as its co-ordinates. I would plot the hazy points on the co-ordinates: no one is alone, horizontally beside each man and co-existing with him is a collectivity of the living. Is this collectivity of his own choosing? Yet everyone expects him to obey it. Moreover, the horizontal collectivity is intersected by a vertical collectivity, concerning which the silence is so complete that one might doubt its existence. Yet how very real it is! And how it dictates to us, and how harsh it is to us, and there is no escape from it and to disobey it is impossible. What freedom it vouchsafes to us, however, for when it drives us to shooting, to suicide, to anything and everything, we exclaim nonetheless: That is what I have decided!

As I reflected thus, suddenly, out of the blue, I felt my temper rising; I shunted my chair ominously in the direction of the chummy Director, and when he inclined his affable ear towards me, I did not spit in it as I was moved to do, but I remarked:

"Well now, how's the family, quite well, quite well?"

"Oh yes, not too bad," he replied with unconstrained alacrity.

"And the boy? The boy's behaving himself?"

"Oh yes, not too bad. He's got his own head now, he's a big boy."

"Sure, you're a big boy too," I said in Prague dialect, so he should understand.

He understood, the rascal! Had I then risen and taken action, I believe he might even have grasped that by my hand he had been dealt a blow by my great-great-grandad the Kuman in person. Unfortunately, however, I had not had enough drink, not nearly enough, and really I have mentioned this incident purely as proof that I was not the least bit drunk. It was merely that I seemed to be getting malaria.

I assumed the freedom to proceed in·the person of my father.

We rose from beneath the tree, we had to move on, although I had a premonition that once we had left we should never return, even if I cried about it. This woman beside me is my son's wife and my son is in the army. And as we walked away from the tall fir tree, I realized that I had set great hopes on this moment, anticipating it as a last chance for a meeting with my dear wife who failed, however, to come. This, then, was the end.

"You know, we used to trail up here every winter through the snow, your husband and I, to fetch a Christmas tree," I told my son's wife.

"He has your legs. He goes to all lengths to get things," she said.

Until this day I had always believed that my son had married a wife who was far too rationally minded, unnecessarily mature. Now I see that I knew her incompletely. She is running ahead of me now down the hill, jumping over the young birches, nearby someone is hammering the blade of a scythe and the sound comes right into the wood. My legs started running after her.

"This, my lass, is the place for me. I'd wish to die here, too, if I had my way."

Silently plucking raspberries in the holt, she offered them to me. I bent and took them straight from her palm with my lips. She looked at me. I took her head in my hands and kissed her on the forehead.

"Die?" she said. "Hm! You'll be here a long time yet!"

"Did you see any cows up there?"

The fellow was wearing a white shirt and a black hat shaded his old face. I knew him.

"No, we didn't see them, Mr Shenkerik."

He shifted his hat and took a closer look at me.

"So it's you? I'd not have known you," he said and he stood there.

"But I saw them. Up among the birches," she said.

He looked at my son's wife.

"Thank'ee," he said to her and to me he added: "Now that's another story. Good day to you."

"Fare thee well," I said to him, although I felt no real anger. It would be more true to say that his suspicion had quickened my pulse.

She, having noticed nothing, again ran ahead. When I came up to her, she turned towards me and I saw she wished to talk once more about my son.

"I knew it, but I could never have imagined how very true it is – you know, he's exactly like you!"

"Really? Now I'm right glad to hear that!"

"But that's just what I'm not, you see! I'd like him to be gooder than you, when he's that old."

Everything was lost again. I showed her where Tarandova lay, and I said that up there, on the ridge, we once had land. Now the bellflowers were blooming all around on the meadow.

11

Snow is falling now on those hills and uplands where once in summertime I walked with my son's wife and the bellflowers were in bloom. There is no view, only the snow driven by the wind over the icy surface. With the gusts of wind the snow rings as it enters through the chinks into the byre where I have decided, after a long climb, to take shelter, make a fire, roast potatoes and arrange my thoughts. All this, save for the last, was soon done, and the last I am unlikely to manage in the time allotted to me. I have heaped up a considerable store of brushwood and fuel. Within an hour the fire is flickering and the chinks to the windward are covered with brushwood, causing a big snowdrift, from which remarkable warmth results in the byre. I have changed my underwear, my trousers and boots are drying and the ski straps are thawing. The blissful feeling of security and safety is illustrated by the sound of bells borne here alternately from the left and the right flanks of the range of hills, from villages higher up towards the Slovak border. People are going after church to their dinners and my eyes happen to fall upon the beam above the door of the byre, where there stands written in blue-wash: *Praise be to Jesus!* Animals differ from people in being unable to think or speak. From that I judge that the greeting is intended for humans in the byre. I respond to it in spirit, and I do so for the same reason as that which has always caused people in these parts to exchange greetings when they meet, whether they know one another or not.

Dressed again in my dry clothes, my ski-gear waxed,

I rejoice in blissful repose upon the dry beech leaves. I occupy myself with reflection and memories. Gradually I am coming to the view that everything is in some way bound up with deep-lying causes. Maybe it is the place where I spent my childhood years herding the cows that shapes my thoughts. Maybe this, too, led me to travel so far with her to pick the raspberries that time before our marriage. That silent, lonely tree is still here today, burdened with snow, the tree under which we were quietly sitting when, with a glance from eye to eye, we made the final decision. And maybe for the self-same reason I would always come in later years with my eldest to seek the Christmas tree in this place. Here, too, I brought his wife one summer in the midst of the hay-making in these hills whence the carts carried the hay down to Tarandova, when my own wife was here no more to walk this earth. Everything was finished.

The clearings are beautiful with their snowy load and their silent beauty. I drive my skis almost reverently through their depths and I abandon myself to memories in the white half-light. I have travelled this way several times this winter. Always the same reasons lead me, those which led me here with my son's wife. Then and now.

I start beyond our stream and in the early morning I make tracks for the ridges of the White Carpathians as far as the spot where we were that time in the summer when the farmer asked us about the cows that had strayed among the birches, and then I turn sharply downhill between the rows of fruit trees, which number 34 rows of 42 trees. Throughout the run down I think about the wife. About my wife and son and his wife again with her son, and in that first pair of loved ones I see the second pair of former days. Alas, it has all gone from me! I wonder whether ever again I shall be able to tickle a little child's belly with my chin.

"What is that you are bringing me, Mother?" my wife asked her Mother.

"A shift for him in the box, if he is to die," her Mother replied.

"But he'll not die," my wife, declared and she was afraid to breathe a word of this event to me until the lad had recovered. And just now I have remembered that he wrote me a letter, but I expect I owe him an answer, because owing to my condition, phantasmagoria, I am unable to get round to doing anything. And now he is almost a complete stranger, and it is only because I see him and hear him in the snatches of time that I have become accustomed to think of him as being the same, although in reality he is a different person, but I still think he is the same, yet he has changed. I wonder if I shall still manage to visit Prague, and I imagine seeing her again with her bent head and how I kiss her thoughtful brow. I think, too, about the difference between her and my daughter, until not long ago my dear daughter and I fell out on this account. Forgetful of where I am, I run on to a deep track buried in powdery snow. My skis sink in and a headlong fall of eleven paces shatters the fairy tale and brings me back to reality, a reality in which I have no wish to stand up again. Indeed, I made no attempt to do so, but strove to clarify the situation which had arisen from my dreaming. It was necessary to remove the snow and to dry myself in the byre.

There is much that I have on my mind, but I cannot tell it to anyone and I no longer possess the detailed patience required for writing. The latest events have caused my people at home to think all sorts of things and, apparently, without regard to what I myself think. They keep puzzling how it is possible for a man to be sick and yet to walk about, roaming in the woods and over the hills. At Christmas time I broke my ribs, three of them, in Hluboko Wood, owing to lack of snow. Packing up my gear, I set out for home, the sun was still shining then. I slipped with both feet on the log surface of the woodland path and fell flat on my back, thereby suffering concussion. That is, when I came to myself the moon was shining, and great was my astonishment. I proceeded homewards, taking about one and a half hours. First they treated my ribs, then they sent me to the psychiatric department in Olomouc. Owing to a shortage of beds, they discharged me after three days with the recommendation: peace, cheerful thoughts and treatment at a spa. Should that prove unsuccessful, arrangements for retirement to be initiated. This they dictated to a typist in my presence, and at that I had no wish to go home, but there seemed to be no non-violent way out. The District Health Commission, which somehow called me in rather quickly for examination, confirmed the hospital's finding and recommended, besides a stay at Podebrady Spa, a process of gradual suicide at home in the kitchen. This I could not bear and with the aid of those who, despite everything, were still my friends after I had been dropped from official posts at district headquarters, I received a booking for treatment almost immediately. It remained to arrange matters at my present place of employment in the factory, where they obliged and they appointed my deputy with remarkable speed. They all want to have me off their hands. When, after my wife's death, I urgently needed a deputy to enable me to have treatment as early as possible, I was unable to obtain anyone for twenty-two weeks . . .

"How did she die?" I asked Dad when I arrived home and had her coffin opened.

"I think the end was not easy, and there was no one with her," he replied in a dry voice and he nailed down the coffin lid again.

I had noticed that a little dry blood remained around her nostrils. Immediately it was borne in upon me that we must all die like that – in public institutions, because our new-type man will not allow it to happen at home. What are crêches for? Why, of course, that we may grow accustomed to the fact that we shall meet our end in modern institutions. However, I said nothing to Dad ...

Dear children!

My hopes of being able to visit you in Prague, or of your coming here, have vanished. I have been sent for treatment to a different place than the one they promised me originally. And I had hoped that discussion would take place between us which could have a decisive influence on the future ordering of my life. Further, I wanted to consult you on property matters, for although you have decided that my daughter shall move into our cottage that we built, your mother and I, well and good, but it is my desire that access to it should not be barred to any of you. I would like to know that any child of ours can be free to pick flowers there, to trample the grass or to gather fruit. But by your silence you have decided. My youngest son and I were no longer able to keep house together, although he bore with me bravely. My fair-haired daughter alone decided to save me and the outcome of her endeavour has been that following the unrest at work I have gained unrest at home as well, while in addition I myself paid for the moving in. Kismet. My treatment here consists of carbon dioxide baths with galvanization of the head and is to last three weeks. I have been fitted out quite nicely with things from home. At meals, except breakfast, I wear a blue suit. Otherwise I have provided myself with a track suit in the Youth League colour, there was no other. Those grey trousers I had last year are at the cleaner's. At home I pruned all the trees before I left. There is nobody to do it, my youngest son is not interested, he is good for nothing. I am lodged in a house on the banks of the river which, when the snow thaws, will rise up by eight feet. Now it is tame and green. I like flood waters and after meals I often spend many hours standing here in solitude. As to my health, I have no better indication than what is obvious – for the present I come up against a brick wall everywhere. I wonder when it will end. To my disadvantage is the fact that after winter spring will come, and I shall have to get down to work. As for a job and earning money, I can announce with a smile that since I no longer provide for anyone, I am assessed as a single man and am treated accordingly on the pay sheets. That depresses me and I fear that it has a corresponding effect on my health. Before coming to the spa I bought soft wood, 3 metres for 300 crowns, 2 metres of hard for 300 crowns. Further, 32 hundredweight of hard coal for 625 crowns. In anticipation of your coming from Prague on holiday and our not having even enough straw palliasses, I had two sets of mattresses made. And for my clothes for the spa I paid 450 crowns. It happened to me that when I fell ill last year, due to deductions from my pay packet I could not repay the cost of the oil paint and the decorating in the kitchen nor of the plumbing that had been done earlier. These sums were still outstanding when the currency reform came and now I am incapable of polishing them off. When balancing the accounts for building works at the factory I also drew up a balance sheet of my personal affairs and since I have been robbing Peter to pay Paul I only then discovered what debts I actually have and that they are many and various. At this discovery my nerve broke and I succumbed to panic. It happened on Christmas Eve, and therefore I set out on a Christmas ski trip to seek some mischance. It turned out badly, for I broke my ribs and injured my head, which, as everyone will agree, offers no way out. They explained matters to me at the psychiatric department in Olomouc. And so I am beginning again, having achieved no more than a worsening of my situation by being unfit for work. I could have paid off a lot of my debts. So now you know, my dears, how I came to be here. My problem is to find a completely new order for my life. To go away – not to go away – where to? My blood pressure has dropped quite a bit and I am on a diet to set me up. I have no friends here, nor do I seek any. It may be that my nature is so bad that it is difficult for me to get acquainted and make friends, though when I was working at the district I never noticed this difficulty and there were many anxious to have me as a friend. No one is going to make me retire in a hurry. I have a strong will and it is necessary to hold out. Please talk these matters over, my dears, you are both wise people and the eldest. And you, wife of my son, you owe me answers to a lot of things . . .

Naturally, on reading the letter, my first thought was that I must talk to Dad at once, but somehow it proved impossible to set aside from our pay the money for the journey to Moravia, which costs quite a lot. But while a way could have been found round that obstacle, I was deterred by the fact that my wife was not so well inclined towards Dad as he imagined her to be. To her his behaviour seemed like that of a madman and my efforts to understand it or find excuses for it irritated her. She was afraid I might be well on the way to being exactly like him in my old age. And for me, in her view, there was far less excuse, because I had not had such a hard life as he had at my age. In the next breath she said, however, who knew what kind of life Dad had really led and whether he had been faithful to Mother out there in foreign parts. Obviously I was painting him in rosy hues in my recollections and I had been his favourite, because my younger brothers, for their part, didn't manage to take the lenient view that I took. Dad had brought his present troubles on himself, nobody wanted to live with him except his daughter, and to cap everything he was horrid to her.

The bellflowers of summer on the upland meadows appeared to figure not at all in my wife's calculations, at the most she was willing to allow that he had been spoilt by other people when he was at the height of his political career. But then, he shouldn't have given in to it. Now he wanted to go traipsing off again to some place, imagining he would escape something, but he would never escape because his torment was within him and would remain with him wherever he went. He was horrid to Mother and when she, my wife, was keeping house for him while Mother was in hospital, he was horrid to her, too. Why, even Grandad and Grandma had thought twice about letting Mother marry him, because people said, apparently, that all the men of his family were horrid to their wives. When I asked who had put that into her head, she said I had told it to her before we got married. Dad was putting on a show of mental instability, but if anything should come his way, he would go off quite calmly and get married, his grieving for Mother wasn't so terrible. I asked her whether she had ever mentioned all this to Dad himself. She replied that she had. But it struck me as impossible, because in that case his feeling for her could hardly have been so lyrical and he would not have felt this desire to be with her. At which she said that there was a terrible contradiction in Dad's nature . . .

Here in the byre I am able to take a more detached view of things. Maybe the spa has helped me, if not by the treatment, at least by forcing me to take a rather harder look at my fate, for I had the time to do so. I am not sure, however, whether I was round the bend back in the old days, or whether it has come upon me now, it's all a matter of one's standpoint. My standpoint is snow-white. What have I got for all my work? I say this with no bitterness, it's a question for the oracles. At Easter, with tears from the children, we used to kill the white kids which had been piddling around the kitchen in the warmth from the stove or, when the sun shone, would gambol outside in the yard. Kismet. A dreadful emptiness in the headpiece and altogether a state of mental collapse. It is essential that I should be fit.

In the meantime I am touring the hills as I did before my fall. If there has been any improvement since then, it is that a few more feet of snow have fallen. And so it seems to me at times that things are not quite so hopeless after all and that I shall come out of it all right. But the doctor put it over on our folk at home that they shouldn't let me go, and I feel so good whenever I'm out and about, away from people. I mustn't give them any excuse for bundling me into a car and carrying me off like Vincek from our street, who has never come back again. I don't wear those old trousers of my son's any more, the ones his bottom grew out of and mine hasn't grown into. One Saturday I took the afternoon bus to the terminus and continued on foot across the clearings as far as Pozar. From there it was a thundering run down to the old path, and there at half past eight in the woods in moonlight I tore the trousers. It was a classic run on hard frozen snow. At least I sleep after these tours. When I wake up, I set out on another. I take some potatoes from under the stairs, and when I come upon a stack of wood I make a fire and there's no worry about being hungry. There's nothing to keep me at home, nothing at all. My son-in-law is at work all the time and my youngest son, too, the one who was born when I was working in Iran. When he is on the afternoon shift he sleeps till nine o'clock in the morning. If my grandchildren kick up a din, and they do that, he thrashes them and throws them into the snow. I am deeply grateful to him.

When I consider what has been, I am in no way surprised that I have ended up as I have. It must, however, be admitted that I was dismissed in a manner designed to preserve a proper decorum, although, on the other hand, I am somewhat appalled by the coldness with which my personal tragedy, my wife's death, was included in the calculations. My dear wife could never have guessed what a role she was to play in local politics. How much better I could have borne it if they had stated their objections to my face, instead of that show of considerations for me in my time of sorrow. I have never trumpeted my personal sorrows in the market-place. Now I am more interested in another matter. If I may put it like this, I can thank Providence for enabling me, in this way, to take a detached view of the life I have led hitherto, especially in the period of building socialism. I have been guided by my own desire to contribute to the betterment of society, and I have been guided by the tasks which, to that end, were in part assigned to me and in part of my own choosing. Not wishing to draw any far-reaching conclusions about our affairs, it will be better to keep to my own person. And here I can say without doubt that it has been easier to find scope and freedom for my bad impulses and inclinations than for the good. Where the worse side of my human nature asserted itself there was always a likelihood that it would meet with understanding and be excused, just as long as I was otherwise obedient. But for my good intentions, even the best of them, there was no green light and the barriers of endless red tape all around. To put it bluntly, a man can drink himself under the table at the village inn any day, but with a lofty purpose he would have to make a pilgrimage to Prague, and he would never arrive there because there are a lot of inns on the road. That is not meant to excuse me, I am content with an alibi, for as the saying goes – better a good alibi than a dog's turd . . .

At this point in Dad's monologue, the monologue spoken through myself, I experienced a desire to turn the conversation to a matter upon which our conversations had never touched.

"That time when you had to hand the meadow over to the co-operative, the one we'd had allotted to us not long before, how did you feel?" I asked him in my own mind.

"A far more important plan was at stake than my plan with that meadow. It was my desire that free people, people no longer plagued by greed or warped by drudgery, should labour nobly together on fields held in common. How could I have advocated that, if I had not been capable of such a small sacrifice and discipline?"

"Well and good," I said. "I know you, you were capable of making sacrifices and you were well disciplined. But what did you do with the anger that was in you?"

"What anger was in me?"

"Anger at the other people who didn't want to make sacrifices," I said. "I can imagine it must be a horrible feeling to be rushing enthusiastically into something, convinced that the others are rushing in one's wake, and then to look round and find that they've stayed behind. Can one take it? Doesn't one feel like driving them on with a whip?"

I waited for his answer, and there was none. Therefore I continued.

"Very well, you were capable of sacrificing something, and you were disciplined. But how would you take it if the others preferred to stay as they were and, in short, they merely gave you the credit for your self-sacrifice and your discipline?"

I waited, no answer came, and I tried to imagine how he might have answered.

"No situation of that kind arose. Because the moment I had rushed into it and the others stayed behind, I received instructions about how to proceed. My personal likes or dislikes carried no weight."

"But to an angry man a timely instruction can be especially timely, can't it?" I asked Dad around two o'clock.

I waited, no answer came, and since I did not venture to imagine his reply, it is not recorded here . . .

Here, in our woods, there is plenty of snow, but in the

dales there is mud. One has to travel on foot, or by bus, or by train. So on Wednesday I rode up to the pass for one crown twenty. From there, on foot to Sidonie and up along by the stream. Magnificent frost. Beautiful waterfalls and all kinds of quiet nooks. That stream has its source in Slovakia and once I crossed it with my firstborn when we were out gathering mushrooms. The boy was taken ill, I carried him home on my back. A lot of snow. The undergrowth was an obstacle in skiing. But I managed to reach the Slovak sheepcotes. It was two in the afternoon. I had nothing to eat. The potatoes had frozen in my haversack. I fetched some hay from the loft and bedded down on it in the shelter of the wall, where for a full two hours I sunbathed. There, in the sun's face, a man could die marvellously. Memories of Shakhabdullazim beneath the mighty Demavend Mountain are strong in my mind. At four o'clock I set out to travel even further, towards Vrshatets; after all, I could make it even by night. It was terribly beautiful. Rugged cliffs. The wind whistled as the sun was setting. Alas, on the way back, big, blue shadows lay across my path.

That's the way things are, day after day, occasionally they send an inquiry from the factory about how I am, but that is a mere formality. Tongues are wagging, of course: Just traipsing about the hills, is he? I have plenty of time for reflection. I experience miracles of momentary optimism. But it is clear to me that I could never live with two women, a double life: one within, the other on the surface, for appearances. Furthermore it is clear to me that I must tear away everything there is around me, though as yet I have no idea how to set about it. I am resolved to live here, where we built our home. That decision, too, is now behind me. My one concern is the ordering of my life. I have no intention of letting myself be killed, I must not be upset either by village or domestic affairs. It looks to me as if I shall not give the cottage to my daughter. I am sure that other children of mine will need it too, although of that they are not aware, they are not yet aware. The eldest of my sons believes he can live in Prague, because he doesn't know himself. He bears a strong stamp of this place. My youngest son is a homing type, I fear he will never poke his nose out of the nest, except to do his military service, but he must have a place to come back to. And I cannot go wrong in deciding for my middle son, who is now studying, he has no idea of things and when the time comes and he begins to wake up, he must not find the gate barred. He has always been fond of me, too. One conclusion seems certainly to follow from this: the house will have to be converted for all of them.

Yesterday I could have encountered my great opportunity. I was skiing where the beech wood has been felled. The big, bare bulk of the long ridge forms the frontier with Slovakia. For perhaps two hours I climbed briskly. When I had had enough, I guessed the homeward direction. Visibility was nil. Visibility nil, and it was impossible to judge the gradient of the slope. A biting wind blowing and freezing water falling. Raindrops rolled over the icy crust. Birds, which had evidently ventured to leave the trees in the dale, were suddenly caught up by the wind and borne helplessly away. Not a soul anywhere. In the old days, when someone asked my first son what he was going to be, his reply came as a matter-of-course; "A carpenter!" That was his answer when he was six to ten years old, then it stopped. He did not choose my trade, and none of my sons have chosen it, and I am not sure how I ought to feel about having failed to lead them to my beloved trade. Instead of doing that, I never forced any one of them into anything, for that is what I worked for, that they should not be forced. I cannot tell what to regret most, should I decide to regret. I started the run downhill, bending almost double, and immediately I was startled by a loud cracking. Below a bushy field-boundary stood a byre and I had landed on its roof. The skis had run through the snow and the flimsy shingles, and I was stuck in it up to the knees. Having scraped the snow away, I unfastened the skis and let them fall inside. Then I laboriously broke through the gable of the byre and brought the skis out. Before that I had a smoke. Just then the clouds lifted and I set course by the top of the church. Now the going was good. I carried right on till I reached one headstone in the graveyard, and there I read when my brother had been born and when he died. I took off my skis and lingered in meditation. The conclusion: that I have lived a long time.

12

Not much is left of this brilliant summer afternoon, so far-removed from Dad's sombre winter trek. The white sun has edged in a yellow glow towards the western hills, the shadows are softer in the wooded valleys, the clouds have melted imperceptibly and a faint green light has crept along the skyline. Now I must go down, down to long-lost Tarandova, if I am to get there before dark.

Yesterday evening I dropped in at cousin Karel Balej's place; I alone knew that I really meant to visit them. Karel never believed I would when he invited me. It must be at least ten years since anyone from our cottage has been in theirs. A long time. No, I never supposed they would have forgotten what happened that time between our two families, but I've been coming to the conclusion that compared with what everyone under that roof has gone through since then, they must surely see our quarrel as a pretty trivial affair. They can't, after all, lay the blame for all their troubles at the door of one man, my father. It was all so long ago. Today Uncle Balej is an old, old man, he has long since lost the art of putting words together in any but the familiar sentences, and my aunt had just finished the milking, so she offered me a glass.

"It's a long time since you were here!" she said, and she laughed.

"Yes, it is," I replied.

"What'd bring him here?" said the more spiteful of my two girl cousins.

"He's your cousin, you know," my aunt explained gently.

"Where's Karel?" I asked.

"At the inn, I suppose, where else would he be?" my aunt replied.

"The usual beer swilling," snapped the elder cousin.

"He plays chess there," put in the younger girl, who may yet find a husband.

"From the look of you," came my uncle's slow voice from his seat by the window, "your life isn't as hard as your dad's was. Or is it?"

"No, I can't say it is, Uncle."

"Let him be," my aunt came to my defence. "What's wrong with his finding an easier way to make a living."

"That's what everybody's after," added my elder cousin.

"But I'm saddled with some sort of proceedings against me and not so long ago I nearly lost my job," I explained, trying to cover the embarrassment which I only made worse by this kind of explanation.

They seemed a bit surprised at that. Then the elder cousin said:

"We've never had regular jobs at all. We just get taken on for the winter, and when spring comes – out you go!"

"Oh, the lasses, they're just girls! But what about that poor boy Karel?" sighed my aunt. "Just hiring himself out by the day!"

"None of your snivelling now, women!" my uncle exclaimed. "What's it to do with him?"

"That's right. Better not to think," said the younger cousin, and with a smile she went into the other room where the blue light soon shone from the television screen.

"How much are the cows giving?" I asked, really wanting to know.

"Would you like some more?" my aunt leant towards me.

"No, no thank you. I just wondered."

"When we use them for carting, it's not so good. Otherwise, one gives ten litres, the other a bit less."

"That's not so bad," I said.

"It's not enough!" cried Uncle. "But in the *kolkhoz,* now, they'd be reckoned as exceptional even so!"

I was relieved to see Karel had arrived.

"Here he is! You invite someone, and then . . ." my aunt turned on him.

"Hullo there!" Karel blundered over, holding out his massive paw. "I wondered if you'd come."

As the clasp of his hand was but a fraction of the force he could exert, so his growling voice held the muted tones of a roar, and a voice like that was disquieting. From that moment all the others in the kitchen fell silent, either because they considered themselves relieved of the duty to carry on a conversation, or they felt they had lost the right to do so now that the leading character had arrived.

"Did you win?" I asked.

"Yes, I won. But looking at it another way, I've lost – all but my soul, that is."

Uncle shifted uneasily in his chair.

"Now dear, you might like to play him something," my aunt intervened hastily. "What about that? You go and play to him." She smiled, and the wrinkles folded, unbelievably, just as my mother's used to fold.

It was with a strange feeling that I followed Karel into the hallway, where a pail of parboiled spuds steamed the air, and the clammy smell of mouldy walls, flaking white-wash and dry rot was carried by the draught from the cellar door. The cream was quietly floating to the surface in the big earthenware milk-pan. My cousin led me upstairs to the attic, opened a door, switched on the light and stood aside to let me go in first.

"Nice place you've got here."

"None of the others are allowed to set foot here. I sweep up for myself, too – meaning I don't bother."

"I see you don't make the bed either."

Pointing out the various corners to me, he said:

"Sit down, or lie down, as you like." He pushed an old

chair with a carved back towards me. "They shoved these things up here," he told me as he stretched out on the antique bed with its high head-board. "And they bought that factory-made trash for themselves."

"And otherwise, what do you do?" I inquired.

"I'm drifting gradually towards old age, observing the collapse of the old values and seeing nothing to take their place, as your sort would write, and it would be nonsense, because my life today is devoid even of the tragic notes."

"Well, how would you write it yourself?"

"Here lies the futile figure of Karel Balej – but I never pick up a pen anyhow; now, if you need a chap to chop wood, cart away some rubbish, empty the cesspool, kill a copper, it's all for a fiver!"

"I meant really, where do you work?"

"Here and there," he spoke deliberately now. "I'm not looking for a steady job. No dolt's ever again going to be in a position to say: Mr Balej, hand in your tools and get out! And the law? say I to this dolt. The law's no concern of yours, says he. So one set of laws doesn't concern me, and ten other laws hunt me down like a dog!"

"You ought to have lodged a complaint – on principle."

"You're joking," smiled my cousin on the bed. "That fellow hadn't an ounce of respect for the law, but the gentry let him stay. And I'm to complain to them? To put it baldly – as the hovels outside its walls stink, so does the castle!"

"You're right there," I said.

"So you see, I don't complain – on principle. But the women are always sending complaints, all over the place." He pointed his thumb to the floor through which we could hear the muffled sound of the television. "I prefer to enjoy the luxury, when I'm called to an office, of slamming the doors until the glass flies."

"But they told me at the Council office that no one would stand in the way of your getting a job now."

"If the people who stood in my way said that, then

they've changed their tune, but the arse on the office chair is the same. I've no time for offices like that."

"You're right there," I said, with a happy feeling.

"They've offered me a job at the brewery – well, I turned it down."

"Why?"

"They're a foul-mouthed lot there."

"Look here, Karel, do you think you may take to the bottle in the end?"

"No, I won't do that. You have to keep fit for my kind of life. And I have a purpose of a sort – to watch them drinking themselves into the ditch. It won't be long now."

Only when I had seen where his sweeping moral gesture ended did it dawn on me what I ought to say to him.

"I travel round the country and I see all these young people growing up. They hate the things you hate. And they'll need people they can look to for an example. But you'll be on the rocks."

"Ste-e-ady now!" He raised his arm from the bed in a gesture towards where I sat and gazed at the ceiling. "I could have been a member of the co-op by now, with a pair of fine horses, or I could be driving a tractor, I could even be an agronomist or something ... why, I might have been the Chairman by now! These days, in our country, all doors are open to the working man. All but one, and I leave it to you, my intellectual cousin, to say what that one is – so you see!"

"I hardly like to put it into words, but surely things are beginning to change, to get better. What do you think?"

"That's your view, is it? Not mine. And let me warn you against good omens, because time in its mercy wafts everything away, including the follies of our local co-operative farm, as the wind wafts the thistledown, and then – who knows when the rain will fall and thousands more thistles will spring up all over the place. Seeing that the times favour the crasser side of man – as you like, but count me out!"

Thus spoke that cousin about whom strange tales were current in these parts, and I could not help but be fascinated. Sometimes I wonder what would have become of me if I hadn't left home, hadn't gone off to study, if I hadn't experienced a different way of life, hadn't become what I am now – if I had spent all those years here. I've never found the answer. But now I say to myself – I'd want, at least, to be like cousin Karel. I would hold my head high and we would be friends. He would join me as the second man in my boycotting.

"But tell me," I said, "where can someone who thinks like you expect to find a solution?"

"Nowhere," and with this word he indicated the blueprint for the quarrels that would have broken into our friendship.

"I doubt if I could live like that. How do you manage?"

He veiled his face once more with the mask of scorn for those not present and said:

"An ancient Scotsman, on his deathbed, admonished his son: 'Never explain, it's useless.' "

Then he rose from the bed, crossed the room to the corner where an upright piano of light-coloured, varnished wood was standing, and lifted the lid.

"You used to sing," he said, "come on now." He started to play, and so I sang:

Oh, Emperor Francis, it's a small land you rule,
Why must you recruit us and not send us to school.
Never fear, lads, the Emperor won't let you grow lean,
Beyond the wide Danube the young rye is green.

I enjoyed the singing and the bit about the land beyond the Danube appealed to me. The piano, too, was interesting; though it looked quite new, it sounded very old.

"Is it new?"

"Yes, five years ago I got it. Paid ten thousand."

"How did you get hold of ten thousand? I've never managed that amount."

"I spent a winter in a logging camp in Slovakia; we slept four to a room." Karel was playing casually as he talked. "One of my room mates was a pretty hard drinker, always coming in plastered and keeping us awake. One night we had such a scrap that I got the wind up and began to take an axe to bed with me. A hard-earned ten thousand, don't you think?"

The sound still puzzled me. I tried several notes separately. The tone had a staccato clarity and a church-like patina.

"Aha!" cried my cousin, "that's all my own work. Of every three strings, I've tightened up each a bit differently – one a mite higher, one lower and the third is just right. So now," he touched the keys, "you see, I have a cart-load of every single tone. I have it for Bach mostly."

Opening the top score on a pile of music, he started playing, and Bach himself would have rejoiced at his spirit. He towered stiffly over the keyboard, shifting his rough fingers awkwardly from key to key and he kept each where it was until it was absolutely necessary elsewhere. The effect was reminiscent of an organ. His rigid frame contorted, he worked up to the final fortissimo which, reverberating through the old house, gradually dissolved into its ancient creaking.

"So you bought yourself a piano!" I marvelled.

"I'll buy one for you if you like, from my next logging job," and there was tenderness in his voice. "You're a bright lad, you'd soon pick up the knack of playing."

"I suppose I would," I agreed. But his thoughts had run off on another tack.

"People round here can buy whatever they want nowadays, so nobody notices anything."

"What don't they notice?"

"That never before in all the world has there been any poverty as strange as ours."

Listening to the motifs he improvised as we talked, it was brought home to me that he and I had attended the same school, had had the same teachers; the tumbledown parts of dry walls where violets grew among the scattered stones, marsh marigolds beside the streams, juniper bushes on the hillsides, bare feet treading the warm mud behind the cows, the lamps unlit of a summer evening, the shabby clothes, the plain farmhouse fare, a pencil a rare possession – was it possible that a man such as he could have stayed for ever in this place? His last school report had been from the middle school; each item of knowledge acquired there had remained for him precise and final, combining within him to provide the admirable corpus of a basic Czech education refined to a rare purity; education as conceived by the head teachers of old with their mastery of copper-plate writing, choral singing, the lore and history of a native land reaching beyond the Danube, of bee-keeping and grafting fruit trees.

To this groundwork time had added nothing, almost nothing more, for time had evidently offered nothing deserving of confidence. And I knew at once what was coming when Karel picked up the five tragic keys; the album opened in my mind and the next moment we were softly intoning the weirdly incongruous verse:

> *Flandern in Not,*
> *durch Flandern reitet der Tod,*
> *Er hat einen weissen Schimmel*
> *wie Cherubin in dem Himmel . . .*

(*Trouble in Flanders/ through Flanders Death rides/ he has a white steed/ like a Cherubim in heaven . . .*)

With the last notes we shook ourselves back to our senses – why sing that of all things? – and yet how indelibly the lines were imprinted on our minds, and we wondered why we had not, at least, hit on the Czech song:

> *Shine, oh golden sun above,*
> *As from my land I now depart,*
> *Warm in this breast the sacred love,*
> *Dry the tears of a grieving heart.*

Perhaps the explanation was simply that we are no longer a nation, merely a docile population. But suddenly it occurred to me to ask Karel:

"Do you think, if it were put to them, that people would rebel?"

"Don't lose any sleep over that, my lad," he replied. "They're just not interested any more. Believe me, the poor have never had it so good as today."

"That's true. Then why are we so gloomy? Do you go to church?" I asked.

"No, I don't. The priest doesn't believe what he preaches."

"The trouble is, we have no philosophy," and, as I spoke, it really seemed to me that we had no philosophy, although Marxism was, of course, fully at our disposal.

"You, I suppose, have your Marxism," Karel remarked.

"That's true," said I, remembering. "I keep forgetting that."

We continued in this vein for a while, until we gradually passed on to the steady decline in the number of feast days and holidays. On Corpus Christi the girls used to scatter flowers along the route of the procession. And Karel recalled how he and his pals had come to blows about a fish down there in the stream that flows through the water meadows. A star-spangled sky arched over the village, a warm and humid night, a night when, so it seemed, we would not be killing a copper. Karel said:

"He'll die of his own accord!"

A mood of calm, undemanding happiness possessed me; we played a few more tunes, sang a few more songs, I was still there, no need to return yet. Fool that I am, I still feel at home in the place. Somehow I always manage to avoid telling myself that my childhood days are there no more and that my birthplace, as I find it now, is carrying some other being in its womb. In a couple of days, when I take the road to the railway station, I shall pass by a cottage where the owners have decided to enlarge their windows.

A veteran bricklayer will be knocking bricks out of the wall, and cousin Karel will be whistling as he mixes the mortar; as he catches sight of me going by with my suitcase, he'll calmly raise a hand in greeting.

As I walked to the station that day, I waved to him, and he, in his sonorous bass, sang me on my way:

> *Dich, mein stilles Tal,*
> *grüss' ich tausendamal . . .*
> (*My quiet valley, I greet you a thousand times*)

And sadly I took my leave of the man who refused to renounce the poorhouse by the stream for a handful of silver, and the dogs can bark at him all they want!

13

Like one of the lilies of the field, my first duty was to acquaint myself with the place where I was to have my being. No one showed me its boundaries. Indeed, no one knows them precisely, because there are no maps. So I chose my own names for the fields, whatever came into my head as I made the rounds: By the Cross, Under the Hill, By the Power Station. This I did before harvest time, so that I could record the yields from the unknown acreage. It seems that I have some 220 acres, of which 55 are under vegetables, with the appropriate number of glasshouses. The vegetable growing is managed for me by an expert who once managed the whole farm, before I came along to take his place. I wonder how he feels about me? Also there are 33 young bullocks for fattening. Now, however, everything must go by the board in order that I may gain the necessary time, for time is what I need.

Since my appointment to this post here, in the area encompassed by a wide sweep of the River Ohre, I have seen little of my youngest son, the one who was born in Iran, except at Party meetings. Some years the crops are ruined by terrible drought, and there are fields that have been lying waste ever since those days when we drove out for all time the enemy of our nation. When my most capable son enrolled with the Youth League for a year on construction work, I discerned immediately that he was motivated primarily by a desire to get out of our cottage, or to be more precise, to get away from me. I smiled to myself. For I saw how quickly he had his things packed, and why not? Then came the day for saying good-bye, when I lent a hand in loading on to the roof of the bus the baggage of this mob, a good two-thirds of them girls. The loudspeakers blared in the street, as did the brass band and everyone in the buses. A frightful pain clenched my brain in an iron grip and when I got home it broke out in full force. I realized that in the meantime all the snow had melted on the hills, and what was I to do?

At first, after my sudden arrival here, I lodged at the hostel where my boy had booked me in, for he really is a good boy. But it was difficult to bear the din kicked up by that gang, coming home at all hours from dances every blessed Saturday and banging doors all down the corridor day in day out. But it was a relief to have a regular routine and meals and nothing to worry about except to keep a normal measure of cleanliness. Also I was at last drawing regular pay, and my constitution being sturdy from our hills, I was able to tackle the day-to-day work without undue fatigue. To work as a farm-hand was soothing. To be sure, the prospect of getting a more responsible post was attractive and in view of the rapid turnover of labour here the chance might come any day. However, everything had to go by the board, in order that I might gain the necessary time. Yet time is short. The lilies, where are they?

Originally there were fifty bullocks, but I tried to get rid of them. I am speaking now of the time when I had accepted the job of manager at an outlying farm. They were out to grass and now and then one of them would take it into its head to play up and we had to go chasing after it over a radius of up to five miles, without any cowboy train-ing or equipment. These whims of theirs interfered with everyone's work, they damaged my health and the health of the cowherds, two women, and therefore I had a patch of barley behind the sheds cut and fenced in, by which means I obtained a run for the bullocks. In bad weather they can shelter in the sheds and also be watered. It is better this way also because there are some big trees where they used to graze, a variety of alder. Very old. My four-legged charges used to seek the shade of these trees in hot weather or when it was raining. Some thoughtful soul however, had burnt out the insides of several of these trees. One of them fell during a storm and it killed one of my bullocks. I can well do without things like that; now the Prosecutor is laying a charge against me. Being unable to succeed in having the trees fenced off, I'm not allowing any grazing there. Three weeks after I started on this job, the roof collapsed in the brewery where the young cattle were being temporarily housed and I had been unable to succeed in having them taken elsewhere. The fallen roof suffocated 13 two-year-old heifers, that meat was usable, we got one out alive and it was three days before another fifteen were found. The herdsman had not counted heads, and this herd as handed over to me was numbered pre-cisely: one herd. Incessant rain made a successful harvest impossible. Rape, that dreadful plant, caused me much suffering. Since the crop was nearly ready for cutting and I had had no experience with it, I was anxious and kept a careful watch. Why, I even read a handbook about how to stook it. It took three self-binders nine days to cut those five acres of rape. One of the machines fell to pieces. And after all that, we had to leave whole strips uncut because some lazy fellow had scattered fertilizer unevenly over the field. It rained and the tractor drivers who were carting the crop refused to interrupt their work in order to take the soaking wet people home. Lucky that I was not armed. For the threshing we had four combines, but they got bogged down and had to be hauled out by a caterpillar tractor. The people sent from the factory to help refused to lift a finger once they had earned a bit, because their firm was making up their wages. I had to watch their every step, above all to make sure that the sacks of rape were not left out on the field overnight. We did the drying in the mill, but people were tired, so they slept instead of turning the wet crop and it fermented. In seventy-four hours I got only five hours sleep in bed. I couldn't stand still, because if I did, I fell asleep. So far I have no living quarters, or, actually, I have, but I have twice been moved out. Every Tuesday I go to a meeting of the Party committee for the estate and every Friday evening to the neighbouring farm where I am their instructor. The comrades are behind-hand with the farm work and also in the field of political work. During the battle for the rape, however, I did not go there at all. I have to cycle five miles to get there. The last time, when I was riding back from a meeting, someone fired at me from a copse and hit me in the calf of my left leg. I managed to ride away and our carter helped me to get the shot out, but I really couldn't find the time to report the matter to the police. We have stacked all the second hay crop to the amount of twenty-five tons, and the straw is in stacks, too. Being unable to plough back the straw, I applied for fifty soldiers with trucks and over Sunday they got it stacked for me. Unfortunately, the accountant refused to authorize the barrel of beer for them, so I had to pay for it myself. We have finished threshing 260 hundred-weight of grain and 234 of rape. In a stack on the field I have a waggon-load of mixed fodder well stored. The grain needs turning over and cleaning. When my mind turns to home, I miss the golden-headed lily, it doesn't grow here on this plain. Where are you all? On the vege-table plots, where we have three horses working, they were falling behind with the work. I managed to get twenty-seven helpers from the Barrandov film studios and they actually saved the situation for me. The people from the Praga Motor Works, on the other hand, turned out sur-prisingly badly. There were constant rows with them and I was often called in to make peace. They had to be taught how to do every job and even after that one had to keep a close eye on them. One of the girls went off to a hay field with a horse-drawn rake, saying that she knew what to do. All right, if you know what to do! Not a bit of it! As she was taking the implement to the field, a sow ran in front of

177

the horse, which took fright. The piglets followed their mother right in front of the wheels and in a moment of panic the girl stamped on the lever that lowers the rake and the piglets were dragged under its teeth. In jumping to hold the horse I broke my spectacles, which caused me much inconvenience, and the compensation for the damage is being negotiated. I shall feel it in my pay packet, there were four of those piglets. I sent two of the girls to stack the fodder mixture. The weather being exceptionally fine, they lay down in the grass. Towards evening I cycled over there to arrange for them to be given a lift home, only to find them fast asleep and the sun was sinking in the west. In the meantime, someone had stolen the tools. Thirty people stood there bawling at me and intending, so they said, to punch my nose, because in the darkness of my heart I had chalked up the damage to the girls' account. I had to call the police and those people got not a penny. The departmental manager beat a retreat and the accountant took leave of us, declaring that he couldn't work with all that noise. I am the only one who can. I still haven't any proper quarters.

I am supposed to live in the house near the vegetable plots. But the former manager, my predecessor, has twice thrown my things out through the door, and he has put four of the girls into my office, where I was to have slept as well, thus making me, in their eyes, into their arch enemy. The fact of the matter is, however, that after taking over the farm documents I refused to sign his work-sheets because the record of jobs done was always illegible while the payment supposed to be due was quite clear. They had been accustomed here to pay for work that no one had done. I said to him on that occasion: "Kindly write the money as illegibly as you write the jobs, then we might arrive at the correct amount to be paid!" What was more, this gentleman had turned the place into a sort of family concern, with all his relatives making easy money, and the farm going to the dogs. Likewise I forbade the carter to drive the mechanics around of an evening to God knows where because there are no inns near here. Then I checked up on the kitchen and I discovered that in July the cook's family had been having meals without paying for the vouchers. I hinted to the cook what I thought about her behaviour, but I was afraid to take the matter any further, for should she decide to quit, I would be in a real fix. And because I made an on-the-spot payment of bonuses to the carters who were shifting the fodder for me day and night, the other employees proceeded to send out petitions all over the place, protesting that I was discriminating in favour of the carters. And yesterday the estate director and the chairman of the works council and a representative of the regional trade-union council turned up here, and the argument lasted from ten o'clock in the morning to three in the afternoon when the vegetable squad with their foreman were out to mob me until, with the use of only the mildest degree of force, I chucked them out into the yard, where they screamed and yelled until a heavy shower drove them away. I still don't know what the outcome will be, but I shall put up a fight through the Party's district committee where I have good friends. But I can't think where my suitcase and my clothes can be. I am wearing my grey pants, my best shoes, a brown jacket and a pullover. And, of course, I have my briefcase with papers and my youngest son's bicycle. My own bicycle is somewhere or other together with that new tyre I had on it. On the whole, I keep in good spirits, so long as they are not dampened by the weather, which is an outright dictator. At least I can manage to sleep anywhere, but there is no place where I can read and I would like to read more about philosophical matters, by Marx. Also, to have the companionship of someone who knows how to caress with hand or eyes. Home? That has gone. I have no home, lest it be with her beneath the sod.

My eldest son has visited me and in his opinion my things are in a mess. But that is my kind of order. We had no real opportunity to talk in peace. I live with the feeling that all my relationships with my children need to be discussed and we never get round to the discussion. My youngest son brought me some of my things from his labour camp and he apologized for not being able to keep in touch with me so much now that we live far apart and also now he is paying attentions to one of the girls there. Real good boys they are, and the youngest is the best of all. It is purely on their account that I have accepted political work and I shall give them no cause to be ashamed of me. The one thing that grieves me is that, though I am working, I find no pleasure in it, but I must not allow things to get on top of me. I cannot find the explanation for this state of affairs merely by looking into it here, and to try and trace the causes higher up, that is beyond me. Now everything must go by the board in order that I may gain the necessary time . . .

He was always saying that he wanted to gain the necessary time. Time for what? that was a mystery to me. And I dared not ask because he obviously thought it was as clear as noonday. He had arrived at a stage when his talk was either a litany of bare figures about costs and yields, or an imparting of mysterious tidings.

I approached his farm over an upland plain desiccated by August; a sharp, greyish sheen was settling flatly on the land, dust rose from the reddened grass beneath my feet, and even from a distance the scattered buildings looked dilapidated. I was amazed to find how utterly alien the landscape appeared; this was my first encounter with such an alien landscape in our country. I was moved by conflicting impressions – of the monumentality and the poverty of the place. Everything suggested that this should be fertile soil, yet according to another everything, it yielded but little. The river, flowing in grand sweeping curves through the clay and fragmented stones, left the soil untouched by its moisture, as though the very water were dry.

I had arrived at last, after many invitations. I must see the place, he had insisted, it would transport me, I would be in transports. Twice I had announced my visit, only to call it off because I had lacked the wherewithal for the fare. Following a path through a cherry orchard, where straying cattle had wrought havoc with the trees, I came to a hillock. The curve of land below me appeared like an oasis. A yellow farmyard nestled up to the bushy hillside. The level strip between the slope and the river glittered with the glass of greenhouses and seed frames. Automatic sprayers were turning this way and that, spreading their dewy mist over the field. Seating myself beneath a withered cherry tree, I gazed into the valley, hoping, with one strong look and an intensive imagining myself into the farmyard, to divine its nature and see everything beforehand. But finding the task beyond my powers, I merely looked and repeated to myself several times : Here at last you have found your orchard and here you have acquired your meadow.

Then I walked slowly down the hill, and as though I were passing through the cave of time into another world, a rock wall must have closed with a light swish behind me, for when I looked back all I saw was a flat, alien horizon, an opaque alien sky and, from far, far away, the sun of our memory, illuminating this place, like that star. Here, to the world of an extinct nation, it bears but a legend of how once upon a time we had a house beneath the lindens where there lived a father and a mother and the others, their children, and neighbours passed our gate on their way to the fields or to the railway station and they spoke to us, while over in the woods, streams flowed and birds sang.

I was approaching the gate into the yard when someone wobbled out on a bicycle. This someone turned out to be Dad. He jumped to the ground, let the bike fall, threw himself upon me and embraced me, and he sighed. He smelt of old coat, straw and tobacco, and as I held him I realized that he had grown smaller. When we had finished, he stepped back, holding me at arm's length.

"You've come. You're here," he said sadly, because there could be no happy sequel to the words. For of our own folk there were none in this house, and the wall crumbling there among the nettles in the reddish light of the setting sun was strange to us, and it was beneath an unfriendly roof that he and I would sleep that night.

We went into the yard. Someone's rough tongue was addressing the cattle in a nearby shed, a gipsy fellow was stumbling past with a pail of mash and he made no response to my greeting. From the two-storeyed building a little girl with yellow plaits came running towards us and she slipped her hand without a word into my father's hand. And so we entered the house.

In the evening a strong white electric bulb shone over the big kitchen table, and I had to stare at its furrowed surface in order to be able to accept the simple fact that anyone here could have such a big, clean table. When a few sulky farm-hands came for their supper, they stood by a hatch in the door, their food was dispensed to them across its shelf, and there they also placed the empty plates.

"Aren't they allowed in here, or what?" I asked Dad, who was having his meal with me at the big table.

"I can't explain in a few words why they can't come in," he replied. "You'll have to take my word for it that I could never have got down to work here at all if I hadn't made a few rules like that."

And he embarked on a long-winded, rambling account of the farm work, while the cook served the other people, then gave supper to the child, then cleared away and only when all was clean and tidy, did she sit down to her own meal.

"Mam, would you be so kind as to make coffee for me and my son?" Dad requested.

I had exchanged no more than a few cursory remarks with the cook. I had the feeling that she would be impatient of any interruption. She was a deft worker and the child helped her in small ways. When Dad had made his request – and I was astounded by the tone of it – I had the impression that she was laughing to herself. And since she was quick to notice a hint of laughter on my part, too, and that I had seen her smile, there flashed between us a split second of understanding which spoke more clearly than any words. But it was not until she brought my coffee that I observed with surprise that the woman was trembling with agitation.

"What's the matter with her?" I asked Dad when she had left the room.

"To that only the Delphic oracle can provide you with an answer," he said.

Later he took me up to his living quarters and office. It was ridiculously touching to see, standing in the middle of that big room, a table, a chair, a bed covered with an army blanket, and that was all. Even his clothes were still in his suitcase. Part of the floor was occupied by documents, pamphlets on farming, and rolls of plans and graphs. Leaving aside the suitcase, which was familiar to me, there was nothing to recall our far-away home in that other world – he had brought nothing with him. A mere trifle betrayed his past: a few numbers of *World of the Soviets* were lying in their remembered order on the windowsill.

Tomorrow morning, when I awake, he will show me round the farm. Now he was leading me to a little room on the other side of the house. He gave me a torch, because someone had ripped the electric wiring from the wall. Four beds were crammed into the room. I asked who usually occupied the place.

"Since I've been expecting you and your family, nobody's been allowed in here," he replied.

"Well, good night," I said.

"And the same to you," he said as he left me.

The night was incredibly black, not a star twinkling. A dry wind sent a restless quivering through the rafters and the branches of old trees scratched at the walls of the house. I lay there and my aching spirit held no distinct thoughts, but a train of heavy, unformed impressions and images passed in slow procession. I was disheartened by having understood so little of what I had seen that day, and the darkness filled me with apprehension. When I admitted them, I was visited by aural hallucinations: I heard rumbling carts drawn by cows, barn doors creaked and a barefooted runner gasped for breath. It even occurred to me that I might never rise from that bed; outstretched and composed, I submitted in all humility to the danger. I am in the hands of my father, the father about whom I am beginning to be clear on one point: he is dead. His life, in which I, too, have lived, ended in that other world. He might just as well have been laid to rest, and that this was not so was due solely to his obduracy. And having outlived his funeral, being a man without an ounce of respect for the death of his life, he was carrying on as though he were alive. He had even invited me to visit this other abode of his; after all, in him my father would always be present; tomorrow he would show me everything and then he would let me go. And one day, quite simply, he would not let me go.

That's not true! My thoughts were not so çlear-cut at the time. I was conscious, then, of no more than a deep anxiety about my father's second life. I was upset and startled on discovering that I was losing Dad again, having believed once already that I had survived the loss. And I had a strong suspicion that the next time, too, it would not be over and done with, since it had not been accomplished once and for all. All this was slowly merging into fear of the outer darkness whence, through the window, came the broad murmuring of the dark river bordering this realm . . .

The weary autumn has passed and now winter is here again, and February, at which time, last year, I did most of my skiing on our hillsides. All that is over and long past.

On his last visit my son said that I was living in a mess, but that was simply my kind of order and I am writing in last year's diary from the beginning again, because at this time last year I had nothing to write about apart from the snow. Everything was already at an end by then and I am glad that I knew it was so. But it would have been beneath a man's dignity to commit self-slaughter, although, on the other hand, I wanted to be sure that I didn't lack the resolve to end it all, and so I conscientiously did all I could to enable the decision to be reached without me, and I would acquiesce. Well, I survived, and if to live is to be my political duty, I shall accept it as the will of Kismet. The cook, Mrs Drahushe, caught a skin disease from the cattle. She had to be isolated. It was hard on the little girl. Luckily, there was no cooking to be done, because the kitchen had been closed. I treated the calves myself, using rubber gloves and chlorinated lime. In the case of Mrs Drahushe, it was not possible to observe these precautions so precisely and therefore my wrist became infected. I wrote to my daughter informing her of my intention that I was about to get married so that she might send me my certificates. Within fourteen days she sent me the feather bedding and the things I had asked for. Now it appears that Drahushe has no certificates, that she isn't actually divorced. Her former husband is living with a woman and he has never bothered about getting a divorce. And so our valley was at one moment like the tower of Babel, the next like a week in the silent house, and at times it was like a migration of nations. The little girl was upset. Her mother wanted to stuff the Christmas presents, two sets of warm underwear, into the furnace. The atmosphere improved somewhat when I had attended a meeting at our headquarters and I got back late at night. She was on the lookout for me, yelling into the darkness, and when I arrived she collapsed. I must say, this struck me as suspicious. I did what I could to revive her, but she had lost her memory. She didn't recognize me and screamed to be allowed to go to me. I didn't want to call a doctor. They would have taken her away, but what about the child?

After this shock, she told me everything. How before my arrival it had been rumoured that I was a tough customer, and so our friend the former manager and his lot had decided to smoke me out or, rather, not to let me settle down at all. When that failed, they began to lay other plans. In a moment of drunkenness, they had bragged about them in her presence, whereupon she became interested in me, this dangerous character. They all moved out, leaving her to keep them informed about me. I must admit that I had my suspicions from the outset. I treated her with considerable coolness, also in view of the advice to that effect which my eldest son gave me when he came from Prague to see me. She had noticed his attitude and was very upset by it. Now I am sick, having worked for two nights on planning costs for the whole year. If I had just the cattle, there'd be no problem. But to foresee all the operations with twenty-two varieties of vegetables is difficult even for a market-gardener. On Monday a considerable blizzard visited this land of the ancient barrow civilization, and I had no telephone connection with the outside world. Yet whenever the work is held up it means interrupting the increase of meat supplies for which people are queuing up. I walked, there was no telephone link. And on the way home I somehow managed to end up on my back on the sunken pathway above the power station. The little girl was with me. She never stirs from my side. She ran screaming to the power station, and the lads carted me home. By morning I had spoken volumes, it seems, but there was no telephone. Mrs Drahushe had wanted to get me to town with the horses, but the little one wouldn't hear of it, so the doctor visited me in the afternoon. I have a bad cold and pain in the whole of my lower jaw, head and ears. Tea, black coffee, a cool-sheeted bed and their combined tears restored me to life.

The little one never stirs from my side, except to go downstairs to tell her mother how I am doing, and conversely. After dinner, Mum in tears! I asked why. "I'm afraid for you," she said, "and now I must tell you why. That time when I was waiting for you and you came so late, I collapsed because I feared you might have been drowned. They were planning to drown you." I was struck dumb. Now, perhaps, we shall discover who shot at me when I was cycling. A fine bunch of rascals! And when my middle son came here from his studies to see me, shortly before the eldest came from Prague, he warned me outright about drowning, and I laughed. Is it possible that his anxiety for his father could be imbued with such foresight? Although the truth is that this middle son of mine is the brightest . . .

My brother, who is now in Slovakia, had been walking behind Dad. With a matter-of-fact eye he surveyed the place and asked:

"Do you often come this way?"

"Only when I'm on foot," Dad replied.

It was a track well trodden in a useful beeline, because it followed the path of the covered channel carrying water to the turbine at the power station. The surrounding land was overgrown with bushes, and the fields beyond were muddy. An ill-humoured autumnal wind puffed up the tails of Dad's green ulster, fleeting gleams from the ineffective sun roamed the turfy hillside beyond the river, the sky was black with the promise of snow.

My brother said something. Dad, not catching the words from behind, turned his head.

"I said: 'Do you come this way at night?' " my brother repeated.

"Yes, I do," replied Dad in the green ulster with the wind worrying at its tails. And he clutched his hat.

"Come over here, Dad," said my brother.

So he walked five paces back. My brother, who is now in Slovakia, was standing astride a big metal plate which covered an opening to the water-course and the current roared beneath him. Screwing up both eyes, he smiled under the peak of his waterproof cap and said:

"That'd be a fine joke."

The channel is three metres wide and it holds two metres of swiftly flowing water. I gave no sign in Mrs Drahuše's presence, but when she had left, I straightaway wrote a deposition charging the watchman with condoning the theft of twenty bundles of tarboard. I observe that I cannot relax as I would wish, to avoid fighting all the time, since it is obviously a fight to the finish. When I haul one of them over the coals, five others start squealing. It's still the revolution here, they've slept through February 1948,[1] and now I'm waking them up. My eldest son was shocked at my harsh way of dealing with some of the people. Where has the devil landed me again! I was looking for peace and quiet, not a load of worries. I have received a rebuke from the Party, so far without any financial sanctions, on account of the brewery collapsing on the cattle, and for having taken it upon myself to hand out a bonus to the carters, although in the first instance there was nothing I could have done about it, while in the second I did the only possible thing. It seems to me, therefore, that to do nothing and to do something add up to the same thing in the end. These are, however, personal incidents in the great endeavour. I asked the people at headquarters to send me, at last, one of the Hungarians, with whom, in any case, they could never come to any understanding. They granted my request and when the fellow had been here two days, very capable, he drew an advance of 160 crowns, he bought himself some rum, smashed up the bar at the inn, and so we had to get rid of him. But during the two days he was with us, he helped with weighing the bullocks, because the records showed I

1 The postwar coalition government in Czechoslovakia ran into crisis, in February 1948. The Communist Party, emerging as the ruling party, proceeded to speed up the programme of nationalization of industry and to introduce the Soviet model in the economy and in all fields of life. The Socialist revolution is officially considered to date from this time.

had a deficit of two tons in beef cattle. Although it was mid-year before I took over the farm, they decreed that it was my business to make up the deficit, so I demanded a check-weighing of the cattle. The Hungarian tied two bullocks up by the trough to the same staple. One lay down while the other was standing with its legs over the head of the first. When this one stood up, it lifted the other, thereby strangling the animal by the neck. The case is with the Prosecutor. I am behind with the February plan. Drahushe keeps crying. If only she had her papers, I would marry her right away, I in my ulster and she in her trench-coat. I have to laugh when I think of my son's wife who once said to me while walking among the moon daisies on the hills, that in men of my type there is always the lover but not so much of the father. I have to laugh when I recall how she prescribed for me among the bell-flowers, saying that it would be good for me to get married and to take a wife from a different part of the country. Mrs Drahushe was wiping my table and seeing the snapshots under the glass, she said to my Prague son: "You weren't nice to me! You there in the glasses, you turned up your nose at me!" That is how she speaks to the photographs and I'm upset about it. Her own family kicked her out because her mother had her by another man. Now they hate her even more for having taken up with a man who has come here to work and to uphold the gains of the working-class struggle. At the moment, our affairs stand as follows: when my eldest son was here and he warned me off this woman, I was not living with Mrs Drahushe, although everybody thought I was. Following the explanation of all the tangled and, in parts, horrifying circumstances enveloping this place, I have been living with her and it's the real thing. I feel like a man who has come in from the rain. I enjoy the order and the warmth of family life. Now everything must go by the board, in order that I may gain the necessary time. I have the love of two people, only time is so short. Mrs Drahushe has all the qualities of a wife: she sends me to fetch the washing from the loft, where she is afraid to go. Further I am required, if I am going that way, to bring milk from the village. Further, she buys my cigarettes and keeps a check on me. As a reliable expert she has the little girl, who says on the steps when I come home:

"Daddy, breathe on me."

A well-regulated life.

These were Dad's thoughts in the house beside the Salmon River and he had no presentiment that within a few years that ancient Celtic vale would be transformed into the bottom of a lake.

14

I had stepped out of my fifth-floor flat and was going down the stairs. From a distance I saw that two black hats were ascending towards me from the depths. When they drew nearer, I moved aside to let them pass. The bobbing black hats stopped and tilted upwards in agitation. Revealed beneath them were two faces red with exertion.

"Hallo there," said the cousins from Tarandova.

"Why, hallo!" I replied. I was exceedingly surprised.

"We'll send some bricklayers, right away, tomorrow, to knock off two stories. This place is too high up," the younger remarked.

"Very good. So we'll clear our things out . . ."

"No need for that, why put yourself out, just use your head!" the older cousin flared up. "We'll knock out the two bottom floors!"

The two of them occupy fairly important posts of some kind in a building concern, but not so important as to prevent them in any way from having labour and material at their beck and call for a bit of moonlighting. There was about an hour to go before the funeral, so without stopping to sit and talk, we set out. It transpired that the cousins had paid for a big wreath at the florist's, which we had to fetch, and then we waited for a tramcar. They were worried about how we should manage to squeeze in among the crowd with our wreath, but I had always noticed that wreaths are carried outside, on a hook at the back of the last car. Hastily we put ours in place, while the conductor observed us through the glass, waiting to ring the bell.

We stood on the platform of the car, my wife sat by the door. The elder of the cousins propped himself against the brake-wheel, and when it rotated under him, he said:

"Whoa, steady now, or we'll be late."

"Look, you clear off to the back, keep away from us," the younger admonished him. He was looking tired from lack of sleep, because they had spent the night in the train.

"But there's a brake at the other end, too," I said.

"Yes indeed, who knows," the younger added, "what would happen if we put both the brakes on, one of us at each end, on which side would the tram pull up?"

"We'd smash it, in any case, each putting on the brake on a different side," said the elder.

"No! We'd squash it!"

"Please don't quarrel," I implored them.

"Whose quarrelling?" the elder retorted, "He's impudent."

The conductor with half-moon spectacles gave us our tickets and remarked:

"I wonder, gentlemen, if you're going to a funeral or a wedding?"

My wife laughed, turning her face from the people in the tram towards the open door, under which dust swirled. The cousins ignored the conductor, and the younger, with a scandalized grimace, complained to me:

"What's the idea here, people poking their noses into other folks' business?"

"It's not my fault," I said and it was true.

After the cremation, we returned to our place. The business of door-closing and hanging up hats was slow, our hearts weren't in it. We went into the room where we have a table in the middle. The cousins took opposite sides of the table, they pulled out chairs and seated themselves as though in unfamiliar, almost official premises. Only two were present, the third is in prison. After a perfunctory touch to their black ties, they placed their hands on the cloth and turned their round, faded eyes in my direction.

Suddenly their faces fell sadly and the elder's voice was low as he asked:

"What happened to Uncle?"

When we got his note telling us that he was in a Prague hospital, though I was puzzled about his being in Prague, I supposed it must be some fairly conventional accident, possibly serious, but understandable in view of his precarious way of life. Not a bit of it.

I was walking down the long corridor, scrutinizing the numbers on the doors, when I glimpsed him standing at the end, smoking. His head was swathed like a Muslim; for a second I thought there might be cause for a primitive joke.

"You've come," he said gravely, "so you've come."

"Of course I've come," I replied, and then it struck me that he really wanted to know why I had come alone.

"The children are ill," I said.

"Which children? Your children. Come this way, I'm supposed to lie down. Drahushe won't be coming now."

I experienced what it feels like when you suddenly discover that you are not wanted as much as you had imagined you were. I hoped he hadn't got the letter I had written three days before.

"Did you get my letter? I wrote to you."

"No, I didn't. It'll be at the farm. Drahushe is sure to bring it."

Perhaps she won't, I thought. Then I listened to his story. His headaches had become so bad that he couldn't even sleep. He had been lurching from one side of the room to the other and at times, during the last four days, his sight failed. He had the feeling that the screen of trees round the house had burst over-soon into leaf, the shadows fell across the window, too. The doctor took one look, and packed him off in an ambulance to the hospital. They told him, sir . . .

"Sir, there must be something in your brain, and it's difficult for us to see in there."

"Comrade head physician," he replied, "I have read in the magazine *World of the Soviets* that in one of the Prague hospitals there's a team of enterprising doctors who are introducing Soviet methods. They know how to open up the skull and look inside."

"You would be willing to undergo that?" the head physician asked.

"Am I still worth it? That's the question!"

Dear Dad, it was out of the question for us to come and see you. The kids are being ill in turns, but the main thing is that I cannot represent our family at your wedding. You are starting a new chapter, you have a right to it, that is in order. But for me, and perhaps for all your children, it is another matter. I cannot witness your marriage and I cannot assist at the ceremony.

I have picked out this letter from his papers, and as I read what I wrote then, I am shocked to find I was incapable of showing more tact. More tact, at least! Not to mention how, a mere five years ago, I could have been so . . . childish, so immature. The relentless lines continue:

There is one Mother, and one alone. This woman – she is a stranger, a good woman maybe, but a stranger. And since you are, of course, going your own way, I can but wish that it will turn out well for you, but for me you are now a different person, less close to me.

If only it had, at least, occurred to me to write – another person, a person with a sequel which I am incapable of following, I cannot, I cannot.

It is the past that binds us, you and me, *I wrote*, and now you have one present, I another. The life of two people is, among other things, a matter of conflict. By dying first, Mother gained an advantage and a moral superiority over you in this conflict – there can be no

194

criticism, it is the best that is remembered. By the laws of nature and of society you are under no obligation to remain with her, but I can, so why shouldn't I?

Of course! Why shouldn't I, when it cost me so little. I swear to God that never before in all my life had I ventured to write anything with such sincerity and such brutal frankness, but why, of all things, did I have to hit upon it in that last letter to him! Yet I cannot entirely condemn my attitude at that time; I still retain something of the fear I felt then and which drove me to write those words in the hope of blocking the road to the slippery slope I guessed must lie ahead.

You are surprised – *my letter continued* – that my "thoughtful wife" has not answered your letter. I have talked to her about that. She has not written because she doesn't want to say anything unkind to you. She agrees with your present decision, but not with your previous actions. She was shocked, you really can't conceive how deeply, by the way things were among us at home, and now she is watching anxiously for signs of whatever I may have inherited from you or acquired by my upbringing. It's getting on my nerves! I wanted her to write to you about it herself because she would have put it more precisely and more delicately, too. For now, I will end, the worst has been said. Dear Dad, all the best to you. With all my heart I wish you well. And I shall be glad to come, later and for other reasons. When you've got it over.

Today, when it is over for him, I cannot conceive that anyone could actually have to read a letter like that on his deathbed. It seems too much like something out of a novel about a relentless fate. But I have duly noted the time schedule in the periodic balancing of accounts, and I shall await with interest the rhythm in my own case.

After the opening of his skull he felt better and his sight was restored.

"I saw him, that executioner of mine!" he told me with respectful admiration and he fluttered his eyelids. He gave me a detailed account of the operation, and whenever his eyes closed with fatigue, he dropped into the dialect; when he opened his eyes again, he spoke in standard Czech.

"They told me, sit down, it won't hurt, but it did hurt, it hurt ... with this delicate file they filed and he says, easy now, now a little more. An energetic young chap he is, you know, young! Young chap – cut off my head if you want, so long as it helps. I was happy to have him do it."

In the midst of complaints about getting food but nothing to drink, about having to lie in bed without raising his head, and having diarrhoea, he launched into a song of praise about what a wonderful and progressive hospital it was and be damned to the people at the farm. At the neighbouring bedside a woman was offering the patient someone's telephone number, she was chatting merrily about nothing in particular.

He fell silent. Without turning to look that way, he said:

"What happy people, to have a telephone number."

After this remark, I left.

On my second visit I found him in bed, and Mrs Drahushe was sitting beside him reading aloud the letter I had written. This time, my first impression on entering the room was that all the heaviness from all the beds was gravitating towards the corner where he lay.

At first, he took no notice of me. But not for the reason I supposed. Never before had I seen him so tired. Nor had I dreamt that the cruel and convulsive dog-weariness I had been accustomed to see occasionally in his face was not yet the real thing, the total fatigue. Perhaps, in those days, it was weakness stiffened in emergency by a dogged obsession, perhaps anger at the exhaustion, or a painful realization that he could do no more, for the time being. This, however, this was collapse. The moment I saw it, it wrung my heart, so that also, for the first time, I experienced what it means to have one's heart wrung. I told myself that whatever superstition might decree, I must ask the doctor whether the condition was really as I saw it. Today, I am surprised by yet another aspect of my behaviour: that I so innocently obeyed the notice about visiting hours and failed to grasp that in every well-run institution visitors are admitted at any time to patients such as he was. They may, in fact, have expected me to come. But I kept to the Sundays and Wednesdays, allowing him to come to fruition there according to the time limit of agricultural science. One more week, and who, dear wife, will do the mowing for you?

On this second visit, he spoke spontaneously, fluently and languidly, without looking at us. Mrs Drahushe wept and she used her own handkerchief to wipe his mouth from time to time. Did she love him? Had he salvaged for her a few good weeks in that rough environment? She was younger and slighter than Mother, thin, tougher, and judging by appearances, more enduring. Her glance at me was scared. My opinion about her had changed, I admitted to myself that she had probably read that letter to him because she had felt that she ought not to keep anything back, and not with any malicious intent.

"Those co-o-ows and calves of mine, all that's so fa-a-ar away," he mumbled faintly out of the corner of his mouth, "but I'll be back there some time, only I haven't got the energy any more . . ."

"What haven't you got?" she asked, bending her tearful face towards him.

"The energy, dammit," he scolded in an undertone.

She had brought him fruit, chocolate and flowers.

"And here's a new pair of pyjamas," she slipped the packet into the locker.

"It doesn't matter," he said, "they'll soon be covered in shit."

He tried to turn over, she helped him, he wanted to see

the flowers. She watched him, glancing from him back to the tulips, and she smiled.

"See there, see," she said, "we've lots of them in the garden . . ."

I noticed, however, how his eyes clung to the light fragile sprays of budding birch leaves, which the florist had added in plenty.

"I'd like," he said.

"What would you like?" I asked.

"You'd never guess," he assumed, mistakenly.

He wanted to lie on the grass at home.

"Children, just keep away from bed, that's a dangerous place," he began the familiar homily. "Compare how many people die in bed and how many at a crossroads. Yet there's a policeman standing at those crossroads and not by the bed."

When an assortment of visitors assembles at a bedside, there is a tacit understanding about the order in which they leave, while one of the number stays to the end of the visiting hour.

I took my leave.

On the third occasion, he was still alone when I arrived, Mrs Drahushe got there a little later, from the station. The moment he saw me, he asked:

"Am I shaved?"

I thought he was asking about his head. It was not bandaged, but had a criss-cross of sticking plaster on one side. I nodded, yes. He didn't laugh and he said with satisfaction:

"That's the comrades."

It was Sunday, he was thinking of his face which was smoothly shaved, and I realized that he could hardly have done it himself. His hands were cold, with pale blotches and blue blotches and somehow dimpled. I had never seen his hands like that before.

At least twice before she arrived, he wanted to be assured that Drahushe would certainly be coming. He looked at her, then fell into a doze. We sat over him in silence.

Suddenly, with a terrific effort, he came to himself and seemed anxious to sit up. She helped him.

"We will discuss the question of my state of health," he said, and after a pause, he continued: "That is what I wanted to say." And he lay down satisfied, having discussed nothing.

"When are you coming home?" she asked ridiculously.

His eyelids drooped wearily.

"You'll have to think that over, won't you?" She stroked his cheek.

He made to prop his head with his hand, but the arm bent like a rag doll's.

"Put your hand so, lean your poor head here," she said, fussing over him.

He opened his eyes and for a precisely allotted time he reverted to happier days with the words:

"I'll thank you to remember I'm a grown man, not a silly little calf!"

She sighed and laughed. It occurs to me, now, that she was actually trying to dispel his dangerous drowsiness.

"And what do the doctors say?" she asked again.

He was silent.

I was overwhelmed by an insistent idea that the last contact with him should be mine, that I had a right to the last genuine discussion, free of any humiliating considerations. Leaving her question unanswered, he simply looked and slowly and purposefully his eyes shifted in my direction. Mrs Drahushe supposed that, as usual, he wouldn't say anything, and unaware that he would, she paid no attention, but let herself be distracted for a while by the conversation around the other beds; she turned to survey the room. Precisely at this moment we were linked behind her back. I was at a loss to know how to grasp this lightning opportunity. It was no use wasting time over trivialities.

"You know?" I articulated soundlessly.

With an absolute clarity and directness unknown in recent years, he spoke silently to me, concluding with words expressed by a gesture of his right hand: he raised it, and over the blanket covering him he drew a derisive cross.

Then he turned his head to the window and to the end of the visit those beautiful blue eyes gazed into the light.

My story was finished – naturally, far shorter and more to the point than here – the cousins relaxed the tense gaze with which they had been listening and allowed it to sink gently to the table. Then they looked at each other in perplexity, the elder shrugged his shoulders helplessly, the younger replied in the same manner and added:

"Ah well. When we get there, we'll have an uncle there. That's supposed to be an advantage these days, isn't it?"

Rising ponderously, my ageing cousins left to catch their train.

Now I am ponderously choosing the exact spot, but it's no longer of such consequence, I am standing on the steep field above Tarandova, that land where man has delved a thousand times is called Kopanka. Barren shoots sprout wildly in all directions from the trunks of ancient trees. Here and there, among the weeds, a grey stalk stands out, bearing a dwarfed ear of rye, the lonely crop which repeats itself here quietly year by year and waits.

I took off my haversack, untied it and, with the axe, I prised off the lid of the urn. Then, pacing the land, I scattered before nightfall. My one remaining wish was for a consolatory blessing, and not finding fitting words on home ground, I turned in a whisper to that far-off land which he could not have forgotten:

Allah-o akbar!

15

I arrived by train, and from the station I walked to a square where a pack of buses was drawn up by the destination boards. I marched past their noses in search of my brother who should have been somewhere there behind the glass. There were two types of vehicle, the older and the newer; at the former I cast only a cursory glance, and on spotting my brother precisely in one of these, I took offence. He was not sitting at the wheel but in the middle of the bus, conversing with his conductress. They had a queue at the doors. When he caught sight of me, he gave an inaudible cry, waved his arms, rushed to his seat, shifted a lever and the doors opened. Close on my heels they shut again.

"See that! He said he'd come, and here he is! This is my brother," he introduced me to the conductress.

"Oh boy, that's what I call a brother!" she complimented me. "And you can see the likeness. Look, swap over!"

"What?" we asked.

"The cap and the glasses," she pointed to his cap and my glasses.

I exchanged my glasses for the driver's cap.

"Why, as alike as two peas!" marvelled the conductress.

"Sure!" said my brother. "And I've another brother besides him!"

"So have I," I said. "He's in Slovakia."

"There's four of you brothers?" In short, the conductress marvelled, but I wouldn't have liked to take over that bag from her.

The queue standing outside worried me.

"Why don't you let them in?" I asked.

"They can wait five minutes," he replied, glancing at his watch.

I often ride on buses, so I have experienced a lot of this sort of thing, but from the outside.

"I didn't know I had a swine for a brother," I remarked.

"Mind your tongue," he warned. "A swine in his off-time!"

"How's that?"

"Like this: we've been waiting here for two hours now according to schedule, but we won't be drawing pay till ten minutes before departure time."

"So why sit here? Hop off home, empty the garbage, feed the chickens."

"Oh yeh, but what if I live at the other end of the route?" he laughed. "And anyhow we haven't any chicks because there's a ban on selling grain in the village."

"Why don't you go to the inn?"

"So I can go to the bad, what! Or am I to sit for two hours nursing a soda?"

"It's been figured out nicely," I said, because here in a nutshell was the denial of all reason. "It's figured out so that the crowd out there will swear at you and at no one else." I pointed to the throng pressing more and more insistently at the doors, quite unaware of being a mob governed by official quarters. Solidly constructed official quarters, at that.

My brother's temper rose. He grabbed my sleeve and dragged me down the aisle between the seats.

"See that? That's what passengers do out of boredom because the bus doesn't leave at once. And there, there and there ..." He pointed to slashed seats, words and geometrical figures carved on the woodwork of the bus.

"What do you expect, they're kids," I said, though it wasn't true.

"But it comes out of my pocket!" my brother fumed.

"How's that?"

"Like this: there's a fixed allowance for maintenance, and if I go over it, I get the basic rate in my pay packet, and that's that!"

"So it's better for the bus to operate in tatters," I said.

"That's it! Or else I'd be drawing just the basic rate."

"Right you are," I said, "and there's the point. It's a principle."

I would like to emphasize that while my brother and I were engaged in this conversation, moving in close proximity to the roots of the spirit of our times, life was carrying on as usual around the bus, the life of this miserable lowland township, every inch of which was decaying and which, having been deprived of the grandeur of the landed estates, had been endowed with no new talent. To a stranger like myself it was only too obvious that this backwater had no aim to lead it forward. And in this place my brother was stuck, in a town which is permitted once a year to have a say in the disposal, at the most, of two brass farthings of its property.

My brother shifted a lever by his seat, the doors opened and the crowd surged into the bus. In their bags they carried the paltry purchases which had acquired a spurious value by virtue of the fact that these people had to come from their villages to do their shopping here, making perhaps three or four attempts before achieving success in the shape of a packet of number ten nails. Oh woe, woe!

"And what you don't yet know," I said, seating myself for the first time in my life on the service seat behind the windscreen, "is that they'll stop giving you your uniforms for free."

"To hell with it!" my brother exclaimed.

"What's that you're sending to hell?" friendly passengers called out in a like dialect, which could not, of course, be fully revealed in this brief sentence.

He merely flapped his hand and turned on the ignition. The floor of the bus quivered and I was possessed by a pleasant excitement. Fact: this was my first taste of sitting behind the windscreen right beside the engine which was lodged under a grooved plastic cover rising from the floor. The conductress clicked her clippers by the doors. Then she called out:

"That's it, driver!"

The driver, my brother, looked left, he looked right and he began to edge the bus slowly forward. He was working busily with hands and legs, shaking only his head in disgust.

"How's that?" he reverted to the matter under discussion. "There's been some talk of it?"

"No. I've worked it out on my own. In all other jobs people have to buy their working clothes. Consequently, your bosses are bound to come up one day with the idea that you should pay for your uniforms. And because you'll turn it down, they'll simply cut your basic rate the next time the wage scales are reviewed. They'll leave you the free uniforms, of course."

"But Christ, they've done that once already! Once, when we complained about low wages, they told us we must count in the free travel and uniforms. Why, that's what they said," my brother objected, as though it was all my fault. We were approaching a crossroads.

"Maybe. But one lot told you that, and the other lot will tell you this. Do you suppose there are still any of the same men on the job?"

"Christ, that's true," he said, furiously changing gear at the crossroads. We had been travelling at a fair speed through the streets of that town.

"But damn it all, that lot said it!" he objected again.

I laughed, really, all I could do was to laugh. But then I took pity on him and tried to explain.

"Look here, the present lot aren't bound in any way by what the others said. That's the whole principle of the thing!"

We were out of the town, my brother was taking things

easy. My mind was still drinking in the fact that it was he who was conveying me, my mind being accustomed to having itself conveyed by public institutions, and here was I being driven by these trustworthy and utterly reliable hands and eyes, as good as my own or better. We raced ahead at top speed. I glanced at my brother's young, pleasing profile, with apple trees flickering behind it and the yellow-bluish plain gliding in the background. Somewhere to the north the legendary Velehrad Castle[1] had been standing for centuries and I was aware that, on the other hand, behind closed lips my brother was savouring one dark, leaden word as coarse as a blanket, a word he hesitated to voice in my presence.

"I sa-a-ay to he-e-ell with it," he hissed as substitute, while behind his teeth rumbled the forbidden word.

After a pause, he asked:

"What's that about a principle?"

"The principle of administration," I said.

"How did you hit on that?"

"Given two points, you can construct a straight line of any length you will."

"And that's a fact!" my brother exclaimed submissively; he spat symbolically under the steering wheel, drove doggedly on for a while, then his face lit up with a most crafty grin.

"But to think that the papers haven't written about it! What sort of a job do you think you're doing with them?" Then, with a brief glance at me, he added indulgently: "Not that you can help it, of course, I suppose you just paste up the copy."

I was pleased by his knowledge and as I was wondering how to explain things to him, I noticed a sign bearing the graphic message that we were approaching a road junction.

1 An ancient castle dating from the Great Moravian Empire (A.D. 870–894); seat of the archbishopric of Moravia, where the Pope sanctioned the use of the Slavonic liturgy in place of the Latin.

"Which way do we go?" I asked.

"Straight on," he replied.

"So you take the turn to the right."

His laugh was knowing as he said with universal validity:

"To hell." After a moment's silence, he added: "Then I'd never get a regular route."

"What route. And whose is this, if not yours?"

"It belongs to a pal of mine. He's been off sick with his stomach for six months now, and it looks like he'll never drive again. It'd suit me down to the ground, seeing I live at one end of it."

We were cruising beautifully, the engine running smoothly, and my ear could detect no fault in its full-throated roar. Of course, we had to make occasional stops, but that was solely because someone needed to alight, having arrived home. This motor running so harmoniously and indomitably inspired me with confidence that everything would turn out well, that some day I, too, would discover an outlet for my strivings.

Finally, my brother reversed the bus into the garage at the house he was temporarily occupying, and at the sight of the great bulk of matter being shifted through the gate, I took the full impact of the almost incredible contradiction: behold, a bus, the very embodiment of corporate dumbness, and behold, here – my live brother!

We entered the house, where we were greeted by his wife who, some years back at a Youth League labour camp in the frontier zone, had made a match of it with my brother and was now rather tremulously rejoicing at my arrival.

"See, and you're not even shaved," she accused her husband.

"Aye, there's worse things than that," said my brother despondently.

As I examined their temporary quarters, I was thinking: In this place they look back upon their enthusiasm. A

door across the passage belonged to another apartment;
my brother told me about their neighbour:

"She switches off the electric motor for the pump down
in the cellar just when we're doing the washing. And when
we have hung out the clothes, she sends her kid to wipe his
dirty hands on them. Sometimes she quietly pulls the key
out of our door and throws it down the lavatory. I don't
like it, so we're saving up for a co-operative apartment."

While he was talking, his wife was watching eagerly for
my surprise. I wagged my head in surprise and repeated:

"Well, that really beats everything!"

"Look you, I'd never bring myself to dirty her washing," my sister-in-law told me, "because that's work
undone. But the keys, I chuck them down the drain whenever she leaves them in the door, otherwise one can't keep
one's end up. And one time I shut her in the cellar, and
he," she pointed to my brother, "he said he'd . . . well, he
scolded me. But I've thought up a fine revenge for when
that scum plays another of her tricks on us. I'm looking
forward to it, I tell you that."

"And she's afraid our neighbour'll lose heart and the
revenge will never come off," my brother laughed.

"Oh no, she'll not lose heart, I'm not worrying," said
my sister-in-law delicately and she asked how hungry I was.

But I wasn't in the least hungry; I took pleasure in her
distinctive, softly uncouth articulation, in the calm little
gestures, the characteristic intonation of her dialect and in
all the gusto with which she consumed everything,
including, no doubt, my giant of a brother.

"Once we'd been out," my brother took up the story,
"and when we got home, the wife said: What shall we
have for supper? Dumpyballs?"

"What?" I asked.

"Dumpyballs," my sister-in-law explained, and her
husband continued.

"So I said, sure, so she mixed the dough and made the
dumpyballs, put melted butter on them and told me:

Grind the poppy-seed. I ground it, and when we scattered it over those dumpyballs . . ."

"They were all purple!" my sister-in-law burst out. "Who'd have thought it! And it was her, she'd taken our key again, and instead of throwing it in the lavatory, she hung on to it and then she sent her brat to grate one of those indelible pencils into our poppy-seed mill. Who ever would have thought of that? And tomorrow I'll tell you some more," said my sister-in-law, whereupon she had to leave for the afternoon shift.

My brother and I sat in front of the television and we talked a bit about music. The reason being that they were showing an international song festival from Warsaw, with ballad singers, male and female, passing in unbroken succession as they plied their repulsive trade. Hermaphrodites, darlings of the adolescents and of the old wives, squawked effeminately into the microphone and my brother found them ridiculous.

"And in winter there aren't any lads to grit the roads," he laughed.

Being without television at home, I was exposed to the full, unblunted impact of the spectacle, in all its unrelieved stupidity. With their curling lips, their pretence of emotions they didn't feel, their banal voices and ready-made melodies, they were just asking for the commentary which my brother and I certainly bestowed on them in good measure.

"You brilliantined dolt," I said to each glossy songster.

"Run off to the *kholkhoz* to hoe the sugar-beet, you plucked goose," was my brother's advice to the songstresses.

A fanatical psychosis of contempt possessed us and we succumbed to it gladly. In it I recognized the real thing, my genuine feeling about these festivals by international troupes of castrated morons and rarified conformist cows. It was so obvious how these goslings were all trying to look different, but since they cherished the same image, the products turned out accordingly, how they all visualized themselves as soloists, how they were anxiously waiting for the welcoming applause as they ambled round a pointless little railing to the microphone, and how under the all-seeing eye of the camera they were at a loss to know what to do even with their tongues. And when I reflected that this mass fatuity, fruit of the principles governing the administration of Europe, including my own country, is allowed to pour forth unchecked from all transmitters, I reached for the only means to which my brother and I, for our part, have free access. When, on the heels of an abysmally vacuous German songstress, a Rumanian star pranced forth on light fantastic toe, lifting her voluminous skirt although there was no mud, I thought to myself, You titty cow! But I was shy of saying it out loud in front of my brother.

"You titty cow!" my brother boomed in disgust, and jumping up, he furiously tugged the television flex out of the socket. "There! And now just you show how you can sing," he said with satisfaction, as if he had switched off the main bamboozler itself, but I knew that the main bamboozler on both sides of the ocean was still at work.

He asked if I was hungry. I said I wasn't, and for a while we talked about music.

"That Smetana and Dvořák, they were a fine pair of idiots, too," my brother remarked.

"I don't think they were, really," I said, after a moment's stunned silence.

"And I think they were," my brother maintained in an off-hand tone, and he added magnanimously: "But you and I can't decide that."

Of course, it was just the sort of opinion I have always expected from this brother of mine, but I had never thought he would argue with me about it. Since there was obviously no hope of reorganizing his system of aesthetic values on the spot, some methodological instruction seemed more in place.

"Now, I don't think they were, you see. And am I an idiot?"

He hesitated before replying.

"Maybe you are, but I don't have to see it."

I shivered with joy.

"There you are, that's just it! The two of us don't have to agree, but would you ever think of banning the performance of Smetana's or Dvořák's works, or of telling them what they should compose?"

"Well, of course I wouldn't," my brother replied, "that's be a crackpot thing to do." And he laughed at the absurdity of the idea.

"And I'd never think of telling you what you can or cannot do with the bus."

"Now on that you're dead right," my brother praised me, "only it isn't everyone can look so self-critically at the next chap, and that'll be the ruin of us, mark my words, I'll fill you up," he took my wine glass and refilled it from a newly opened bottle of the co-op vintage.

I agreed with his view and told him that the director of our newspaper trust was a furrier by trade and had never written anything, not even about how to educate the young.

"I'll give you an example," my brother promised, and he gave it. "I'm allowed to write up twenty-five minutes for C Two. But that C Two actually takes me forty-five minutes! What do you say to that?"

"How do I know what C Two is?"

"It's cleaning the whole inside of the bus, including wiping the seats, washing the floor and cleaning the inside of the windows."

"You can't get that done in twenty-five minutes, that stands to reason."

"And there we are!" cried my brother, jumping up in his excitement and starting to pace the room.

I licked a finger and passed it round the rim of the glass, trying to make it ring. I succeeded.

"Yes, but the main thing is – what to do about it?"

"What can one do?" my brother sighed.

That annoyed me. I, too, jumped up.

"As I said . . ." my brother continued, "it needs writing about."

I knew exactly what he was driving at. There was no point in it, but I'd never get him to believe that. Faith in the power of the printed word dies hard. Were I to start telling him that the drivers could solve the matter only by taking a bus to it, he would merely think that I didn't want to write about it. He would have to taste defeat to the bitter end.

So I said: "Get hold of a typewriter, we'll have it written up in no time."

He said he would look in on the secretary of the local council and arrange to have a machine the next day – for the present . . . pity to spoil the evening. I was somewhat surprised that he could hope to borrow a typewriter in that quarter.

"Bet your life! He'll oblige! I drive the truck on Sundays. The Council has a truck, but it hasn't got a driver."

In five minutes he was back.

"That's fixed," he said with satisfaction. "They're glad I drive the truck sometimes of a Sunday."

For a time we returned to our discussion of cultural matters. And I recalled an incident from childhood. I told him about it. At Grandma's, in the house where I had imagined the Emperor's portrait, one day when I was little, cousin Karel and I were there together. Uncle put a strap round our necks and told us to have a tug-of-war. Karel won.

"Karel is stronger," our uncle announced, "but you're the cleverer."

"He isn't, he isn't!" shouted cousin Karel and he wanted Uncle to put the strap round our necks once more.

"But he is cleverer," our wily Uncle said. "Tell me, lads, what is culture?"

"Culture, that's being educated," I asserted and I looked at Karel who stood dumb with surprise before starting to snigger wildly.

"Educated he says, oh my, so it's being educated," he laughed uproariously, pointing at me. "Where did the fathead get that from?"

I turned indignantly to Uncle, expecting him to stand up for me as was only right and proper, but then I observed that he was softly and irrepressibly chuckling, so much that he couldn't even draw breath between the choking gusts of laughter.

"Tell me, Karel my boy, what culture is," gasped my good uncle, whom I was to understand some decades later and then I began to respect him too.

"Culture, why it's in the woods, the trees!"

I came to the end of my story, my brother laughed in delight and said that what was more, he knew of a magnificent fallen beech about an hour's walk from her, it had been lying there for two years.

We passed the evening in friendly conversation until the time when my brother's wife came home from her shift at work. She inquired immediately what we had had to eat and offered to knock up some balls, which my brother refused on the grounds that, so he said, she might bloody well regret it. So she remarked that we couldn't have had anything to drink because we weren't singing, just talking a hell of a lot. She asked why I hadn't been offered any *slivovitz*, to which I replied that I didn't know why.

"Because you have a saphead and an imbecile for a brother," she explained.

"Saphead he may be, but an imbecile, no – that's not true, I would object to that," I retorted, putting an arm round my brother's neck.

"Let go of me!" He broke away. "An imbecile's what I am, oh yes, and what an imbecile! If I weren't I wouldn't be working for this firm! What I told you about C Two goes for C One as well. Twelve minutes it is in the book, but it takes a good twenty. What's more, I'm paid for doing it once a day, but I have to do it as many as three times. If you don't want to have the passengers swallowing dust, you have to do it three times, but you're paid for once, well, of course, that's the principle."

He shrugged it off and collapsed merrily in a chair, he really didn't care any more, I saw that above all he was glad to have me there.

"Tomorrow we'll write it all down. Think of as many examples like that as you can," I told him.

We talked for a while about world literature, especially about Remarque and his *Three Comrades*, and suddenly we felt a bit sad. Meanwhile, my sister-in-law was having a bath; she came in with her hair freshly combed and wearing a long dressing-gown, she brought us coffee and sat with her legs tucked under her on the sofa. At that moment I realized that my one-time piddling brother who got rotten marks at school and was no good at minding the goats was now not merely the driver of a mighty bus, he was also married just like me or anyone else, he had to send his child to his mother-in-law's so that the two of them could work on variously interweaving shifts in order to get the money for an apartment, that I had known nothing about it all and I was visiting them for the first time, which was incredible. The resolve for which I had needed so long to muster myself seemed in consequence all the better and more justified, and also more promising, and all the mists of whims and moods were suddenly dispersed.

"Now I would like to acquaint you with the state of affairs in the Czechoslovak press," I said, and I asked if they would be interested. They both promptly agreed and my sister-in-law said outright:

"Why, I'm right glad, after all, when does one have a chance of hearing about such things?"

I acquainted them truthfully with the state of affairs in the press.

When I had finished, they both sat for a while in stunned silence, until my sister-in-law slowly shook her head and said:

"Well, I must say, my eyes are popping!"

My brother laughed:

"Well, it's like it is in our transport concern."

"That's it. Believe me, it is," I affirmed.

My brother asked:

"And what about that chap, what did you call him, that Slavek? Did he take back what he'd written in that article?"

"No, he didn't. There, you see, I forgot to tell you the end of that story. Well, he didn't go back on anything, do you want to know why? When the director forced him to go to the factory and apologize to the officials, he went there and discovered that they'd called a big meeting of all employees, so he'd have to apologize in front of the whole lot . . ."

"And Slavek, did he do it?" my brother interrupted.

"He would have, but . . ."

"Well then, he didn't," my brother sighed with relief.

"But first he needed to go to the lavatory, and when he got there he heard some chaps talking about how they wondered what this journalist would say. If he took back what he'd written, then he'd be a chicken, because the article was true."

"But he didn't do it," my sister-in-law assured herself anxiously.

"He didn't, because when he arrived, in the crowded hall, he had a coronary. And he died."

"Come off it," my brother said in dismay.

However, I could but confirm that it was so.

In the ensuing quiet it flashed across my mind that Slavek it was who had once said that in our hands lies the decision as to the degree of prostitution this nation can permit itself. He never guessed that it would be his lot to come up against that norm so fatefully. My sister-in-law stared silently at the floor, while my brother got up and started walking about the room. Then he stopped and said:

"I'll leave the Party."

I considered this.

"Not just yet. Not till I say so."

My sister-in-law, however, shook her head doubtfully, she hesitated and then, after all, she announced:

"Yes but . . . it's an end to socialism anyhow."

My brother collapsed, only managing to wail:

"Fact, you can see it all, even in our firm!"

His wife was incensed:

"But I don't understand . . . what are they doing in Prague, our capital, the brain of the nation!"

I had to laugh.

"It was a mistake, way back in history," said my brother, "when we joined up with the Premysls."[1]

His wife turned scornfully upon him:

"You're being wise after the event!"

I supported her view that one must take things as they are, and with that we began to think about bed. My brother stopped only to find me some old pants of his, a shirt and a jacket, we drank some soda water and went to bed. The prospect of tearing the nation apart doesn't even bear thinking about. I assumed they would put me in the other room, but my sister-in-law retired there, having decided that for this night my brother and I were to be together.

At five o'clock in the morning, as planned, we got up, I put on his old things, quietly we made tea and prepared to slip out, when the door opened and a white sister-in-law in a long nightgown tearfully pleaded:

"Oh boys, don't go, why it's Sunday!"

It was obvious, however, that we would go, for to tell

---

[1] The Premysl family headed the Bohemian tribes which, from A.D. 895 dominated Bohemia and Moravia. Legend has it that this first dynasty of the Czech state was founded by Premysl the Ploughman and Princess Libuse.

the truth I can't see my brother and me responding to her appeal by glancing at each other, pulling off our pants and going back to bed. So when that failed to happen, she asked:

"And what would you like for dinner?"

"Dumpyballs," I replied quickly and my brother sniggered.

We took a coarse saw from the shed, tied a rope round it and set forth.

At a distance of some three miles, which we had covered before traffic of any kind had time to appear on the road, was the resting place of a long slender beech and it had been resting there for two years. The trunk was not so very thick, but its length required cutting into thirteen sections. My brother's original idea had been to saw off two or three of the best pieces, each of which could be separately and stealthily removed on a handcart, but there, on the spot, not even our combined forces could enable us to shoulder the responsibility for the rest of the trunk, which we would be leaving to rot. And so, having duly sawn off the projected four logs, we seemed to be at the half-way mark. True, we were not there, but since, in the process of considering whether to continue, we did continue, we had then actually reached half-way. And as once long ago, on that day which was ever present in my thoughts, although I had spoken not a word about it, mine was, again, the weaker hand on the saw.

"Let's chuck it in, why bust yourself, you're on holiday," my brother said.

"It doesn't matter," I replied. "Just one more piece."

"But how'm I to get it home? Oh, to hell! I'll take it bit by bit."

"You'll manage somehow," I encouraged him.

"But supposing someone steals it? But why should they!"

"Why should they," I agreed.

Actually, the possibility had been in the back of my

mind all along. History has no message, except for complete idiots.

"Somebody's sure to steal it off me," my brother sighed as he knelt by the tree.

"Well, it's possible," I admitted heavily, though I didn't want to alarm him.

"Or the keeper may find it, it's right under his nose here."

We were not far from the forester's lodge, which was why we had been talking in undertones all day. Moreover, the tree was lying right beside the stream along which ran a woodland path.

My brother was worried.

"Here you are for the first time, and something like this has to crop up."

"Forget it," I comforted him, "they're your pants, after all." I pointed to a knee which I had ripped open as I squatted.

"Do you know who'd have been happy right now?" my brother asked. "Our dad."

Ineffable joy welled up within me, for he could not have spoken a truer word, happiness infused my every pore and wherever it flowed it dissolved the maladies.

We arrived home five hours later than we had promised. My brother's wife had long since lost all pleasure in the dish of dumpyballs she had prepared for us. I was curious to learn what these dumpyballs were.

When we had polished off the dumpyballs, we had to lie down immediately and we slept for three hours.

When we woke up, the sun was in the west and it was high time to start putting together an outline of my brother's protest. Whereupon we were faced – and there was no point in shutting one's eyes to it – by the obvious fact that we could not manage both. If we wrote the protest, we should not be able to shift the timber.

"We'll do the writing, and that's that," my brother cut through the problem at a stroke. "Now you're here, you can help me with it. The timber – I can tackle that alone!"

"Think twice, mate!"

"Christ, you're right there. Somebody's going to steal the lot off me."

"That's what I'm telling you – think it over."

He dropped despairing into a chair.

"Bugger it, what now? Am I to fetch the typewriter or the truck?"

My sister-in-law had been fuming all the time. She said:

"Don't fetch anything – are you crazy or what? Just once in a while your brother comes here and all you can think of is to work him to death. He won't come again!"

This outburst really alarmed me. I visualized the timber to which I had devoted this first visit to my brother being snatched from us by some lazy good-for-nothing.

"I don't know," I told my brother, "you must decide for yourself what you need most."

He seated himself at the table like a reasonable man and concluded that not impulse but a sober examination of the problem was the way to reach a decision.

"Now the protest, that'd be a matter of principle, that's a fact. But then, the timber, that's for my home."

He seemed to have grasped the point, I merely had to relieve him of the worst moment, he was my brother, after all!

"So run and fetch the truck!"

He shot up merrily and was gone.

The light was failing, the truck was standing in front of the house, we got into the old togs again and my sister-in-law scolded:

"Idiot! Your brother'll never come again. You wait till I tell my folks!"

"Don't worry, I'll come back," I soothed her.

"Shut up, you won't!"

"What's the idea, yelling at him! Is he supposed to come back after that?" my brother snapped.

The gilt had melted into thin air, and I saw the issue

confronting me in all its baldness: was I to side with my brother or with a woman who was a stranger to me?

"Please keep out of this," I advised my sister-in-law mildly. "Don't try to preach, this is his affair and mine."

"And what about you?" she turned furiously on my brother, because she couldn't really dare to go too far with me for the time being. "D'you think I'm all that stuck on your brother coming or not coming? He kept clear of us all that time, he can stay away again."

I pretended not to have grasped the full import of her words; I retired to the next room to change my shirt. I could hear my brother trying, in muffled tones, to reason with her.

"You're letting your tongue run away with you. So look out, look out, or I'll smack you."

"Well, I don't care! Do what you like, the two of you. But how'll I be able to show my face in the village if the keeper catches you? And how can I go to Council meetings after that?"

"So that's what's worrying you!" My brother was flabbergasted. "So we can get going right away. We're off!" he shouted to me and left the house.

We had climbed into the driver's cab, he was starting up, when his wife came running. She tapped on the window on my side, I opened the door, she squeezed in beside me wearing an old Youth League blouse, and the truck shot forward.

After all, we had estimated the time badly, instead of the expected twilight, it was almost dark in the woods. We had also estimated badly the negotiable length for the logs and it transpired that we simply could not negotiate them. It was more a matter of rolling and tilting them. I transported them down to the stream and my brother got them up from the stream to the track where our car was standing. His wife kept watch at the junction with the road. Though I thought it unlikely that anyone would spot us. Darkness thickened and the operations were complicated by the fact that one man alone could not manage to lift the logs to the height of the truck. Added to which, my sister-in-law made us all the more jumpy by persistently sending signals of some kind, the purport of which we had no time to ascertain. I had lifted perhaps the tenth log on to the truck, not so much with my hands as with my belly. And with each piece of timber we wallowed through the stream like cattle or dead drunks. And then, for me, the last straw was to find my brother's morale cracking. He had visions of us being caught and exposed to the public eye, and beneath the torrent of his imaginings he groaned even more than I did under the load.

"What'll I do? What'll I do?" he kept numbly repeating the question to which I could give no answer.

"Don't worry," I pacified him, "the keeper's sure to be inefficient."

"Why, tell me why?" he clutched at the hope.

"Because why should keepers particularly be the exceptions?"

"Yes, that's true, do you think it's true?" he wheezed.

It dawned on me that however tough he might be physically in comparison with myself, he was in reality a very severely trounced, down-trodden, and disciplined fellow, a mere civilian compared with a journalist accustomed to the volleys from shit-shooters of varying calibres. What lovely darkness, what a noble cause, what fine timber, what honest toil!

Then, when my dear sister-in-law came running with the news that someone had stepped out of the keeper's lodge and was making in our direction, all I said to myself was, so this is it.

"Come off it! It's not true," my brother tried to reassure himself.

Alas, outlined against the lighter strip of path where it joined the road there loomed, indeed, a human form. For some twenty seconds it peered into the woodland darkness, at us, but not venturing to take a step nearer, it retreated. Of course: our wild, blind squelching in the stream and the thudding of logs on the body of the truck must have been audible half a mile away. But there was no help for it, the logic of things impelled us to carry on laboriously loading the remaining logs, while I was repeatedly telling my brother that he had no cause for fear, that we could make things hot for that keeper – think of letting a tree lie on the ground for two years! And right under his nose! Furthermore it occurred to me that we were not obliged to drive back past the keeper's lodge, we could carry on, circumvent it a bit and make a detour home. But my brother said the detour would amount to fourteen miles. Again, the way he'd been broken in! Then we shut the back of the truck as quietly as possible and climbed into the cab. My brother mounted from his side, his wife from the other, and I, barely managing to make it on my shaky legs, tumbled myself against her sturdy hip. Finally, with bated breath, we all listened in the silent darkness. After which I had to laugh, and I cannot but laugh again today at the memory: for suddenly, into the silence of the woodland, our truck sent forth a full-throated roar and with terrific gruntings and breaking of wind it proceeded as inconspicuously as possible towards the junction with the road. I would count among moments of happiness those fleeting seconds when, in the fullness of physical bliss, a man's noble spirit is perfectly aware of his state and observes it with wise comprehension. Well now, that was the happiness I experienced, quivering with exhaustion while my brother beside me was busily operating all the mechanisms and conveying us with all due caution straight at the keeper's lodge.

Bravely we emerged on to the road. A bit lower down, a bare two hundred yards away, shone the windows of the lodge. My brother, presumably because he was once more in the saddle, reviewed the situation and evidently found it highly promising, because even before all our wheels were on the asphalt, he yelled:

"And now – abracadabra!"

And already we were shooting forward at enormous speed.

"Halloa, a merry ride to the gates of hell, cried Texas Jack," I responded, and from that moment we were living, as it were, on a higher and exalted plane. In the split second of passing the lodge, I glimpsed a car standing there with its lights on. And, as was only to be expected, it was on our tail at once.

"They're after us, lads," my sister-in-law informed us, her head turned to the rear window all the time.

Our engine-room thundered.

My sister-in-law reported:

"They're coming, they're coming, step on it, can't you get any more out of her?"

Within seconds our legs were assailed by a fantastic blast, I could feel the heat creeping between my thighs and hers. The road was straight, tatters of noise lingered far behind us. Ahead, however, a red light was shining and it was drawing closer. I recollected that a section of the road was under repair, reducing the thoroughfare to a single lane. From the opposite direction, meeting us, several pairs of lights were approaching the bottleneck. Maybe my brother never gave it a thought, maybe it is all so much in his blood, anyhow, he careered full tilt into the narrow lane. We got there first, the oncoming lights stopped.

We roared through.

And immediately the bottleneck was jammed with the cars we had met. It was a minute before my sister-in-law announced:

"Now he's through!"

But by then we had shot ahead round a curve in the road and had reached the first buildings of the village. We braked sharply in front of the garages, reversed and somewhat crookedly joined the row of cars parked there for the night. My brother switched off the engine, extinguished the lights, and we sat as quiet as mice. Within about half a minute, lights appeared round the bend. With a faint swish they slid past us to disappear beyond the houses ahead.

I have profited enormously – I have recaptured my native awareness. My next visit will be to my brother in Slovakia.

EUROPEAN CLASSICS